"Because having pancakes when it's not breakfast is fun, right, Sam?"

Again, the boy gr[...] [...]ed with a wink.

Natalie put her h[...] sure how long it [...] replaced, if that's [...] only open for breakfast and lunch, but we'll try."

Des cleared his throat. "I have an idea. I'll follow you to the garage and we'll go to Aunt Polly's while Ogle is checking out your car." What was he doing? Did he just suggest they go to eat? As in *together*? As in a public place? Not only would he be seen in public, but with a woman and her son. Gossip would be flying from one end of town to the next.

She turned to Des, her eyes wide. "Are you sure you don't mind?"

No, he wasn't sure, but he wasn't about to change his mind and disappoint Sam. Still, it wasn't just about Sam, was it? He wanted to spend time with Natalie, plain and simple. But could he do that without falling under her spell?

* * *

SMALL-TOWN SWEETHEARTS:
Small towns, huge passion

Dear Reader,

I wish I could go on and on about the joy of Christmas, but I confess I was able to identify with my hero's scroogeness. I lost two immediate family members at Christmastime, changing it forever. Anyone who has lost a loved one knows the pain fades with the passing of time and new joys work their way into your heart, but holidays are always bittersweet.

I found new reasons to celebrate Christmas and wanted that for Des, but he wants no part of it. That's why single mother Natalie is the perfect heroine for a grump like him—she's as fearless as they come. Plus, she bakes the most delicious Christmas goodies that even a grouch like Des has trouble resisting.

Will Natalie and her young son be able to work their way into Des's closed heart, or has she met her match in *The Scrooge of Loon Lake*?

I'd love to know what you think of my stories. You may email me at carrie@carrienichols.com or visit me on Facebook at www.Facebook.com/authorCarrieNichols.

Carrie Nichols

The Scrooge of Loon Lake

Carrie Nichols

H HARLEQUIN® SPECIAL EDITION

Recycling programs
for this product may
not exist in your area.

ISBN-13: 978-1-335-57420-6

The Scrooge of Loon Lake

Copyright © 2019 by Carol Opalinski

Printed in U.S.A.

Carrie Nichols grew up in New England but moved south and traded snow for central AC. She loves to travel, is addicted to British crime dramas and knows a *Seinfeld* quote appropriate for every occasion.

A 2016 RWA Golden Heart® Award winner and two-time Maggie Award for Excellence winner, she has one tolerant husband, two grown sons and two critical cats. To her dismay, Carrie's characters—like her family—often ignore the wisdom and guidance she offers.

Books by Carrie Nichols

Harlequin Special Edition

Small-Town Sweethearts

The Marine's Secret Daughter
The Sergeant's Unexpected Family
The Scrooge of Loon Lake

This is dedicated to the two Jills.
My agent, Jill Marsal, who believed in my writing voice before I knew how to plot or write conflict, and my walking partner, Jill Ralph, who not only pulls me away from my desk twice a day but is the perfect sounding board for story problems.

Chapter One

Desmond "Des" Gallagher heaved a frustrated sigh as he stared at the scattered pieces of colorful glass laid out on his workbench. This was the third day in a row he'd come to the former business office in the spacious barn he now used as his workshop and done nothing but sit and stare. The scarred and chipped wood that made up the table's surface attested to the fact that work did indeed get done here. Just not today. Or yesterday. He rubbed a hand over the stubble on his face. And not even the day before that. Normally, seeing the glass laid out before him was enough to spark an idea, even if he had no concrete design in mind.

Today's project was an unfinished stained glass window that could be installed in place of an existing window frame or framed and hung like a painting. While those remained popular, his new love was shattered glass sculptures. Shattering the glass himself, he enjoyed taking those broken pieces and creating something new and better from them. Although he'd experimented with small, blown glass items, he'd shunned the much larger ones because crafting those required more than one person.

Having to think about a project stifled his creativity. His best work came when his brain sent signals directly to his fingers and he assembled pieces without conscious thought. Crazy, but who was he to argue with something that had served him well enough to earn a living? He wasn't getting rich from it but his art supplemented his military disability.

Stretching his neck, he scowled. *Christmas.* That was the problem. He couldn't escape the dreaded holiday nor the painful memories the season triggered. He did his best to avoid going into town from Thanksgiving until well into January because Loon Lake loved its Christmas celebrations. Main Street, with its quaint, brick-front shops huddled around the town green, would soon be decked out in lights, garlands and, God help him, holiday cheer. If he couldn't get an item at the gas station mini-mart on the edge of town or by ordering online, he went without until after the holidays.

And what was his excuse for avoiding the town the other ten months? He reached for his stainless-steel insulated mug and took a sip of his favorite Sumatran coffee from beans he'd ground that morning. Yeah, he took his coffee seriously. Maybe if he pretended he *had* an idea one would come. Pfft, talk about clutching at straws. Shaking his head, he set the mug down and reached for the grozier pliers.

"Yoo-hoo? Lieutenant Gallagher?"

His head snapped up at the interruption. A petite blonde woman, dressed in a bright red parka, stood in the doorway. One hand held a red and green tin; the other clutched the hand of a towheaded boy who looked to be about four or five. What the...? He discouraged visitors and studiously shunned community activities to avoid becoming embroiled in the residents' lives—and thereby ensuring they, in turn, stayed out of his.

How did she even find her way out here? He lived in the back of beyond; his fifty-acre former horse farm could be considered isolated, even in a sparsely populated state like Vermont. His nearest neighbor, Brody Wilson, was five miles away and that was as the crow flew. And unlike Brody, Des had no interest in keeping horses, so the numerous paddocks surrounding the barn remained as empty as the day he'd bought the place. Summers working on a dude ranch had cured him of the romance of horse ownership.

The woman, who appeared to be in her mid- to late-twenties, stepped closer. Close enough for a subtle lavender scent to reach him.

"Hi. I was hoping I could have a minute of your time." Her broad smile revealed a crooked bottom tooth.

He had no business noticing that tooth, even less thinking it was...what? Not sexy, but appealing in some wholesome, girl-next-door way. He scowled at his thoughts. "Why? Are my minutes better than yours?"

"Sir?" She shook her head, her long, corn-silk hair

brushing against, and contrasting with, the cherry-red of her jacket. "No. I—I meant—"

"Unless you know something I don't, you taking one of my minutes won't increase yours." He was acting like a first-class jerk, but she'd set off warning bells. And what was the deal with that *sir*? It grated on his nerves. Here he was checking her out and she was addressing him as *sir*. At thirty-four, he couldn't be more than eight or ten years her senior. He sighed. It wasn't her language that had him spooked. No, it was his reaction to her that had him acting like a complete ass.

A small furrow appeared in the middle of her forehead. Damn, but she even frowned cute. That clinched it because he wasn't into *cute*. And certainly not ones who addressed him as *sir. Let it go, Gallagher.* His type might be blondes but they were also tall and blatantly sexy with a mouthful of perfect teeth. That disqualified the five-foot-nothing woman with the crooked tooth. Considering how many women he'd been with in the past three years, though, his type would appear to be fictional women.

Her full bottom lip now hid the tooth and he looked away. He rose from the stool he'd been perched on, careful not to put too much weight on his left leg after sitting for so long. Staggering or collapsing in front of her was not the look he was going for. Ha! She'd probably rush to help and his ego had taken enough beating with the *sir. That's letting it go?*

Bottom line, he needed to get rid of her before she regrouped, started using that killer smile on him again. He hitched his chin at the tin she carried. "If you're here from the town's welcoming committee, you're three years too late."

She shook her head, causing her hair to sway. "That's not why I'm here. I—I saw your work at the General Store and—"

"Then you should've bought it there. I don't sell pieces out of my workshop. Didn't Tavie explain that?" His location wasn't a secret, but the tourists and residents of Loon Lake bought his stuff in town and left him alone, and that was the way he liked it. "How did you even find me?"

"It wasn't easy, believe me." She gave him a tentative smile.

He grunted. "And yet, here you are."

"I can be quite resourceful and frankly—" she glanced around the cavernous barn, empty and scrupulously clean except for his cluttered work area "—it's not exactly some Bond villain's supersecret lair."

Her smile seemed to be an invitation to join in, but he deepened his scowl. It was either that or start grinning foolishly. She was charming, and he remembered he didn't do charming. And, by God, he wouldn't allow himself to *be* charmed.

She licked her lips and swallowed. "Tavie gave me directions."

"That figures," he muttered.

Octavia "Tavie" Whatley might be proprietress of Loon Lake General Store, but general busybody was her true occupation. Not much went on in town without her knowing about it, but she'd sold more of his pieces than anyone, so he grit his teeth and put up with her.

Even with his frugal lifestyle, the military disability only went so far.

"Dear me, where are my manners. I'm Natalie Pierce." She let go of the boy's hand and placed her palm over the top of his head in a tender gesture. "And this is my son, Sam."

The kid grinned up at him, his eyes the same clear August-sky blue as hers. Des nodded to the boy. He had nothing against children. *Just women with bright sunny smiles? And let's not forget that oddly appealing crooked tooth.* Damn. He didn't want or need these distractions. *Yeah, because you're so busy being creative.* He told his nothing-but-trouble inner voice to shut up.

"I hate to interrupt—" she began.

"But you're doing it, anyway." And the jerk behavior continued. Her presence was flustering him so he was repaying the favor. See if he could fluster her a bit. His reaction wasn't her fault, but he was in survival mode because that weaponized smile of hers had scrambled his thought process. He'd gone too long without female company. That was it; blame this on self-imposed celibacy.

"Lieutenant Gallagher, I—"

"Call me Des. My navy days are behind me." His days of being catapulted at one hundred and sixty-five miles an hour from the deck of a carrier in a metal casket worth seventy million dollars were over. He grit his teeth and rubbed his knotted thigh muscles. Why did he want her to call him Des? Saying his given name shouldn't matter because he was trying to get her and that way too appealing smile out of his barn. Wasn't he?

"Des," she said, drawing it out.

"Yeah, but it's generally one short syllable." But her version worked. Worked a bit too well, as a matter of fact.

"Sorry." She inhaled as if she was about to launch into a prepared speech.

He opened his mouth to—

"I'm here to talk to you about handcrafting some items for an auction we're having. Christmas ornaments would be a real hit this time of year. And it's for a great cause. There's this fantastic hippotherapy program that needs—"

"Stop right there." He held up his hand like a cop halting traffic. "Doesn't matter the cause. I don't do Christmas. Period."

"What? No Christmas? But…but… Why?" She blinked owlishly. "What's not to love about Christmas?"

How about being a child and spending it with a suicidal mother? Always worried she would disappear. He would've been left alone because his biological father wanted nothing to do with Des. In his dad's mind, Des was proof of an indiscretion while attending an out-of-town conference. "I have my reasons."

She opened her mouth, but Sam tugged on her sleeve. She looked down, and the boy up, his eyes large and his stare intense, both standing still like they were having a telepathic conversation. One that excluded everyone else, even him. She glanced at her watch, sighed and nodded her head.

"To be honest, it took me much longer than I expected to find this place," she said, gnawing on her bottom lip, calling his attention to it again.

"Maybe that's the way I like it," he said, even though

he wasn't sure if she'd been talking to him, her son or herself. He'd been too distracted by that bottom lip.

She set the tin on the workbench next to his tools. "I have to leave, but I warn you, I don't give up easily, even if you do cloak yourself in that grumpiness like it's a virtue."

The boy tugged on her sleeve in another silent plea and she nodded. There was that nonverbal communication again, reminding Des he wasn't a part of their world. Not that he wanted to be. Nope. Not one little bit.

She took the boy's hand in hers. "I'll be in touch," she said as if it was a threat and headed for the door.

"Wait," he called and she turned her head to look over her shoulder. He pointed at the tin. "What's this?"

"Don't worry, it's not a bomb," she said and smiled briefly. "It's homemade Christmas bark. Even a grinch like you can't say no to that."

"What the heck is…?" He glanced up, but she was gone.

Shaking his head, he opened the tin to reveal irregularly shaped bars of white chocolate covered with red and green M&Ms and crushed candy canes. Grabbing one and taking a large bite, he sank back on the stool and thought about the mystery that was Natalie Pierce. What the heck had just happened? Her soft, lilting voice, coupled with that appealing smile, had taunted him and he wanted to know more about her. Her speech was devoid of the flatter, more nasal vowel tones he'd grown accustomed to since moving here. But neither could he peg her as having a Southern drawl. And the kid hadn't spoken at all, but he'd smiled and made eye contact. Maybe the boy—Sam—was shy. Des shook his head. None of this was his problem, so why was he wasting time on it?

He glanced at the pieces of colorful glass sitting idle on the bench and his fingers itched to create something. He popped the half-eaten piece of candy into his mouth, brushed his palms together and picked up the pliers.

The next morning Des stood and thrust his shoulders back to work out the kinks from sitting hunched over the workbench. He couldn't remember the last time he'd pulled an all-nighter, but he wasn't about to leave and have his muse desert him again. He scratched the scruff on his jaw with his fingertips and glanced at the now-empty tin. Huh. As he'd worked last night, he'd munched on her delicious candy. This stained glass window was of the lake during winter when many of the trees were bare. Up close, the lake and trees were individual pieces, but when standing back, those pieces became shades and ripples of the lake water.

A car door slammed and he scowled as his heart kicked up at the thought that the visitor might be Natalie. Uh-oh. Was she back? Who else could it be? Natalie Pierce had been his only visitor in recent memory. He didn't know whether to be glad or annoyed. He started to rise but his leg and his inner voice protested. *Down, Gallagher. You're not an addict waiting for your dealer.*

It was indeed Natalie Pierce and she was holding her son's hand again. In the other, she carried a plate wrapped in aluminum foil. What did she bring today?

"I told you I'd be back." She smiled, the crooked tooth peeking out.

He quirked an eyebrow. "So I should take your threats seriously?"

"Maybe you should." She laughed.

Heat coursed through his veins at the sound. "Are you in the habit of threatening all the men in your life?"

"Is this your way of asking if I'm married?" she asked with a significant lift of her eyebrows.

Yeah, he was about as subtle as a sidewinder missile. He grunted instead of replying.

"I assure you that Sam is the only man in my life." She showed him her crooked smile. "One thing you need to know about me, Lieutenant. I follow through on my promises."

"Des." He'd enjoyed hearing his name yesterday in that musical voice. Liked it a little too much but he'd worry about that later.

"Des," she repeated and set the plate on a clean corner at the end of the workbench. "I hope you like gingerbread men. They're quintessential Christmas, don't you think?"

He grunted, trying not to give her any encouragement, but his stomach rumbled, reminding him he hadn't had any breakfast yet.

"I used my grandmother's recipe and her forged tin cookie cutter." She let go of the boy's hand and began removing the foil. "They're fresh, but I'll let you in on a little secret. Even after a few days, you can warm them in the microwave and they will have that fresh-from-the-oven taste. Sam likes them best that way. Don't you, Sam?"

She glanced down at the empty space next to her. "Sam?" Her voice rose. "Sam?"

She uttered something under her breath and raced out of the barn. He'd been so fascinated by her mouth as she spoke, he hadn't noticed the boy's disappearing act. But then the kid couldn't have gotten far, and there wasn't anything nearby that could hurt him. Des grabbed a cookie and followed her as quickly as his bum leg allowed.

Natalie's heart hammered as she rushed from the barn. She'd never forgive herself if— She choked back a sob. She was overreacting but couldn't prevent it.

She had no idea Sam was capable of disappearing so fast or so stealthily. He'd overcome many of his balance issues since starting equine-assisted therapy. Another reason she needed to save the program. And as soon as she found him, she'd celebrate his acting like an adventurous five-year-old boy.

She was gasping for air by the time she located him standing next to a sleek, top-of-the-line, black-and-red snowmobile parked on the side of the barn. He must've spotted it on their way in. She'd been so consumed with the prospect of seeing Des again and what she was going to say that she hadn't paid attention to her surroundings. Shame on her.

She didn't know a lot about snowmobiles, but she guessed this one was expensive. "Sam, honey, don't touch."

Not that she could blame Sam for being curious. Weren't all little boys fascinated by that sort of stuff? A lump in her throat threatened to cut off her oxygen. For all of his challenges, and Lord knew there were many, Sam was still like all boys his age. After suffering life-threatening injuries, he'd had to learn to walk again but still had occasional balance issues. She'd been warned that his ability to speak might never return. "Be careful. You could hurt yourself."

"There's not much chance of that."

Natalie turned. The lieutenant bit the head off the gingerbread man in his hand. Was his cavalier attitude toward Sam's safety bugging her, or was it the fact that looking at him had her insides clamoring for…for what? For something she hadn't wanted in such a long time, she had no name for it. But the strange yearning she couldn't name made her want to snarl at him in a primal reaction similar to fight or flight. *Remember you want his help with the auction.* Neither fight nor flight would get her what she wanted for Sam.

"Easy for you to say. He's not your son," she pointed out and grit her teeth, not understanding her reaction to Des Gallagher. Grumpiness aside, he wasn't menacing, despite his disheveled appearance, and yet, he threatened her on some visceral level.

"Even if he was," he said, brushing cookie crumbs off his shirt as if he didn't have a care in the world, "it doesn't change facts."

She narrowed her eyes at Des as if he represented some sort of threat. *He does*, a voice screamed at her. But the danger wasn't physical…well, unless you counted her body's reaction to him. He wasn't her type, she argued with herself. For one thing, he was too tall, at least two or three inches over six feet to her mere five foot two. Okay, okay, five feet and one and a half inches. He couldn't be called charming or even pleasant.

His face was covered in stubble, his eyes a little

bloodshot. He appeared to be wearing the same clothes as yesterday, a red-and-black buffalo-plaid flannel shirt over a cream-colored, waffle-knit shirt and faded jeans. Had he been up all night? Working or drinking?

She was going with *working* because she hadn't smelled any alcohol or even breath mints on him. Besides, Tavie hadn't said anything about a drinking problem, and she would know. Natalie was convinced the owner of Loon Lake General Store knew everything about everyone.

Des muttered something under his breath and limped toward Sam. How come she hadn't noticed that limp before? *Maybe because he'd been sitting down.* As her neighbor's little brother might say, "Duh, Natalie." Being around this man had her on her toes. Too bad being around him also drained IQ points.

"Have you ever been on a snowmobile?" Des hunkered down next to Sam with an exhaled grunt.

What was the matter with his left leg? Was that why he was no longer in the navy? She took back every nasty or unkind thought she'd ever had about Des Gallagher. *Except the thoughts you were thinking last night weren't unkind.* Some might call them *nasty* but with a totally different connotation of that particular word.

Tavie Whatley had talked about Des but hadn't said anything about permanent or debilitating injuries. Was it simple politeness or was Tavie caught under his spell, too?

What's this too *business? I haven't fallen under his spell.*

"This will be our first winter here," she said, hoping to steer her thoughts to more wholesome topics. "We didn't get much snow where we lived before. We're looking forward to real snow, aren't we, Sam?"

His blue eyes wide, Sam nodded enthusiastically.

"Real snow? What other kind is there?" Des snorted and threw her a questioning glance. "Where the heck did you live before?"

"Nashville. We'd get some snow accumulation, but it didn't last much past noon on sunny days. Sam and I are looking forward to building our first snowman, going sledding and having snowball fights."

"Be careful what you wish for," he said. "Along with all those snowmen come shoveling, scraping your car, crappy driving conditions, salt and sand all winter long. To name a few of the exciting perks."

"And yet, here you are." She parroted his words from yesterday and made sure the challenge was evident in her tone.

He made a noise, blowing air through his lips. "Maybe I'm a glutton for punishment."

She laughed. He was enjoying this too much to be as fractious as he wanted her to believe. "I'll bet you enjoy every minute of the snow. The more miserable, the better."

He rolled his eyes. "Remind me not to play poker with you."

She frowned at his comment. Wait, was he groaning? "Why? I don't understand your meaning."

"You see too much." He shook his head. "I predict if we have a bad winter, you'll be crying uncle long before mud season."

"Mud season?"

"It's Vermont's fifth season and comes between winter and spring." He glanced at her sneakers. "You might want to invest in a decent pair of rubber boots before then, not to mention snow boots for the snow you're wanting."

"We're here to stay. It would take more than snow or mud to chase us away." She squared her shoulders and forced strength into her voice. "And that's a promise, not a threat. In case you were wondering."

"Thanks for clearing that up." The side of his mouth lifted a fraction, the only indication he might be amused.

She moved closer and rested her hand on the padded seat of the snowmobile. "I must say, you have an impressive piece of equipment."

"Gee, thanks, it's been a while since anyone has complimented me on my…equipment," he said in a dead pan tone.

She turned toward him. What did she—*Oh!* So much for wholesome. She closed her eyes, wishing the ground would swallow her up because now her imagination was going there. The last time she'd flirted could be measured in years, definitely before her marriage to Ryan. Her face burning up, she opened her eyes and met his gaze. His face was impassive except for an ever-so-slight lift of his eyebrows.

Her mouth opened and closed. Great, she couldn't manage anything except an imitation of a goldfish. His expression didn't change, but she had the distinct feeling he was relishing her discomfort. When she narrowed her eyes at him, he rubbed a hand over his mouth, his fingers making a scratching sound on the stubble. How would those dark whiskers feel against her skin? *Stay away from there, Natalie. You're way out of your depth.*

Okay, so the man had a sense of humor hidden under that ill-mannered exterior. What would he be like if— No, she wanted him to make some ornaments for her auction. That was all. Nothing more. But there was no harm in noticing how his chest filled out that flannel shirt, was there?

"...on a snowmobile before?" Des had been talking to Sam while she'd been daydreaming about things she shouldn't.

Sam, who seemed to be hanging on every word Des said, shook his head. Natalie's chest tightened. Last year her dad had suffered one of those widow-maker heart attacks, and Sam had lost the closest male role model he'd had since his dad and her late husband, Ryan, passed away. Sure, he had plenty of doting women in his life, but she knew they couldn't fill the void the same way a man could. Her father had been a crusty career army drill sergeant but had had a soft spot for Sam she could have hit blindfolded.

She listened as Des explained how the snowmobile worked and she made a mental note to look for a toy one Sam could add to his beloved collection of die-cast miniature cars. It would make a nice stocking stuffer. There wasn't an abundance of extra money for Christmas presents, so she was making sure each gift from Santa was well thought out.

Des rose and stepped back until he stood shoulder to shoulder with her. "He doesn't say much."

She knew she could agree with him and that would be the end of the matter. That was what she'd learned to do with people who passed anonymously through their lives. She'd even perfected her smile when people said things like "I wish mine was that quiet."

"That's because he can't. Three years ago, when Sam was two, a car jumped the curb into a crowd of people leaving a minor league baseball game in Nashville, where we were living. That crowd included my husband and my son. Ryan was killed and Sam suffered a TBI." She cleared her throat. "Sorry, a TBI is—"

"Traumatic brain injury," Des interrupted. "I'm familiar with the term."

She glanced at Sam, who was still enamored with the snowmobile. "I'll spare you all the fancy medical jargon and say he understands words, but his brain can't plan and sequence the movements to say them. *Apraxia of speech* is the official term."

Des nodded. "And this hippotherapy you mentioned helps?"

"Not with speech but it helps with muscle memory and balance," she said. "Plus, he enjoys it. Being with the horses is more of a reward than just another therapy session like with the speech-language pathologists or physical therapy."

"Is that why you left in such a hurry yesterday?"

"Yeah, that's one appointment he doesn't like to miss. Sam, don't climb up there. It's—"

"It's fine. He won't hurt anything," Des interrupted and motioned to Sam. "You can sit on the seat if you want, bud."

Natalie tamped down the automatic protest that sprang up and pressed her lips together. It wasn't easy, but she needed to allow Sam room to explore. Smothering him only helped her, not him.

Des shifted his stance, bringing her attention back to him. She longed to ask what had happened to him, but politeness made her hold her tongue. Telling him she'd noticed his limp seemed a bit too forward, despite his mentioning Sam's lack of verbal skills. Her Southern mother had drilled proper manners into her with the zeal of Natalie's drill sergeant father. Plus, she was enjoying the sunshine on this final day in November. Not to mention being in the company of a male over the age of five. She didn't want to spoil either with awkward questions.

"Is he in school?"

She shook her head. "I held him back an extra year. You can do that with kindergarten. He still had a lot of weekly therapy sessions and he's made great strides in almost everything this year, which was why I felt comfortable enough to pick up and move here."

"So will he ever be able to…" Des trailed off and winced.

"Every individual's recovery is different." Even to herself, her answer sounded rote and unconvincing. "We're working with an AAC device. Sorry, that's his augmentative and alternative communication device. Ha, my dad was career army so I grew up with all those military acronyms, but I must say medical experts love them just as much."

"Ah, an army brat. That explains it." He weighed her with a critical squint.

She shifted under his scrutiny. "Explains what?"

"You have a slight accent, but I haven't been able to place it."

"Yeah, I guess my speech patterns are a mixture

of everywhere. My mom is from Georgia, so I have a bit of her accent but did my best to fit in wherever we were living at the time." Her stomach did a little fluttery thing. He'd tried to pick out her accent? That meant he'd thought about her. A little thing like that shouldn't please her as much as it did. *Why not?* her inner voice demanded, because she'd given him enough thought since yesterday. Des Gallagher had occupied a lot of headspace for such a brief meeting.

His face was impassive, but his gaze roamed over her. "Georgia? Huh, maybe that explains it."

"My accent?"

He shook his head. "Nope."

"Sorry? You've lost me." Her knees wobbled under his examination. What the heck was he on about?

"How old are you?"

"Twenty-six. Why?" She stood straighter. Despite a few silver strands threaded in his thick, lustrously black hair, he seemed no older than his midthirties. They were contemporaries.

He grunted. "There's eight years separating us. Hardly calls for you to *sir* me."

"When did I call you *sir*?" She couldn't recall a faux pas like that.

He rubbed the back of his scalp. "Yesterday. When you first walked in."

"You must have flustered me." *Should I be admitting that?* "Between my drill sergeant father and Southern mother, *sir* and *ma'am* comes naturally. I—I sometimes fall back on that if I feel like I've been put on the spot."

He swiped a hand across his mouth, his dark eyes amused. "In that case, I apologize for flustering you."

"Bless your heart, you can't help it," she said in a perfect imitation of her mother, not that he would know that.

His eyes narrowed in suspicion. "Am I detecting an insult in there somewhere?"

"If you are, then that's on you." Natalie shook her head, doing her best to look innocent. "Are you from Loon Lake?"

"Colorado. I settled here after leaving the navy three years ago."

Her gaze went to his white American foursquare home with its hip roof, black shutters and wide brick steps leading to the front entrance. The house seemed large for one person and she wondered if he'd planned to share it with someone when he'd invested in the property. Tavie had mentioned he lived alone. Again, not her business if he had a dozen girlfriends. "So have I changed your mind about those ornaments?"

"Not a chance, Ms. Pierce." He took a step back as if needing to put distance between them. "Don't waste your time on a lost cause."

Great. She'd managed to kill the camaraderie they'd shared moments ago. She plastered a smile on her face. "I gotta warn you. I'm a champion of lost causes. A regular St. Jude." Holding out her hand, she said, "Come along, Sam, I think we've taken up enough of Lieutenant Gallagher's time for one day."

Chapter Two

Des watched them walk away and felt...what? *Relief, that's what you feel.* He shook his head and limped toward the house. He didn't need or want a woman in his life, especially one with a child. Sam was a cute kid and seemed bright and curious, despite his lack of verbal skills. No, this had nothing to do with Sam. His reluctance was all down to Natalie. She was making him feel things, think about a future he'd given up wanting a long time ago.

Natalie's gingerbread men.

Halfway toward the house, he stopped. That plate of delicious cookies was still on his workbench. Heaving a sigh, he turned back toward the barn. Those were too good to take the chance of some critter getting them. He'd caught a crow hanging around the barn and had

had small items go missing from his workbench. No proof the bird was the thief but he had his suspicions. Yeah, that wasn't crazy or anything.

He retrieved his cookies, eating one on the way back to the house. In his mind's eye he could see Natalie's striking blue eyes, pert nose and Cupid's bow lips that kept forming a smile. From the first words she'd uttered, her voice had grabbed him in the gut…and elsewhere. *Damn.* He needed to stop thinking about the beautiful Natalie Pierce. A blind man could see she was a white-picket-fence-kids-dog-soccer-practice type of woman.

He might have had a similar dream once upon a time, but it died the day he had to punch out of his aircraft. Those three seconds, the most violent experience of his life, had changed the course of his future. That was the amount of time it had taken from pulling the lever until he was under the chute. A textbook low altitude ejection. Except for the part where his parachute lines had gotten twisted and he'd lost precious time correcting them while plummeting toward the earth.

He'd hit the ground hard, shattering his left leg and fracturing his spine. After two surgeries and endless months of PT, he'd regained his ability to walk but not to fly jets. Although Ashley had stuck by him during his recovery, once she realized he'd no longer be flying jets, she began voicing concerns over their engagement. She'd said perhaps they wanted different things from marriage. Evidently being married to him wasn't her dream so much as being the wife of an aviator. Any aviator.

As a last-ditch effort to salvage their relationship, he showed her the horse farm he'd stumbled across and had admired while visiting Riley Cooper in Loon Lake. Stupidly, he had thought maybe the beautiful family home and the prospect of having room for horses would appeal to her. At one time she'd claimed to be a horse lover, but she'd taken one look and said she hadn't signed on to live in small-town Vermont. The place wasn't even on Google Maps for heaven's sake. She'd thought after a career in the navy, he'd work for a major carrier, they'd live in a metropolitan area and would take advantage of all of the travel perks. Yeah, she'd had their future all planned out, except he wasn't sure where his wishes fit in.

Going into the house he'd gone ahead and purchased after their final split, he set the plate of cookies on the counter and slipped another one off the stack. He had a crazy thought that he would never confess under the threat of torture, but he swore he could taste the love Natalie put into her baking. He suspected she put her heart into everything she did. Sam, with his big grin, was proof of that. A woman like Natalie deserved someone who had a heart.

He glanced around at his state-of-the-art kitchen with its stainless-steel appliances, granite countertops and the off-white cabinets with glass inserts on the upper doors. The kitchen had been remodeled by the previous owner. When he and Ashley had toured the house, he'd figured the updated kitchen would be another point in his favor, but like everything else it had gone bust. So for the past three years, he'd rattled around in the immaculate kitchen using the refrigerator, microwave and coffeemaker.

Too bad he had nothing more than a dream kitchen to give a women like Natalie.

* * *

Des set the pliers back down. His new piece had stalled and it had nothing to do with the fact that Natalie hadn't returned for two days. Two days and no cookies, no pleas for him to make something for her auction. He'd listened for the sound of a car but all he heard was the silence. Silence was why he'd chosen this place. He liked silence. Huh, he and Sam would get along fine. It sure beat her chattering nonsense.

And he didn't care if Natalie's blue eyes reminded him of the adrenaline rush he'd gotten—and missed—when successfully landing his jet on the rolling deck of a carrier. He would've sworn there was nothing in the world to compete with going from one hundred and fifty miles an hour to nothing in the two seconds it took for the arresting wires to do their job. But looking into those clear eyes… He shook his head to shake some sense into it. What was he doing thinking that way about this woman? Hadn't he learned his lesson? First his mother, then Ashley. How long would it take for Natalie to see the flaws in him?

His mother still lived in Colorado, in the bungalow he'd grown up in. Although he dutifully called on a regular basis to see if she needed anything, the answer was always no. But he called anyway, just as he'd contacted the man who'd fathered him and been rebuffed. So he lived half a continent away and used his acres as a buffer between him and the rest of the world.

Disgusted with his unproductive thoughts, he got up and put another log into the woodstove in the corner of his work area. They'd had some unusually warm days at the end of November, a truly long autumn, but December had come, bringing much colder temperatures.

Back at his workbench, he held up the piece he'd cut this morning when he'd first come to his workroom. The curve of the glass still wasn't to his exacting standards. He'd have to redo it. Again. Maybe he should abandon adding the loon—except he'd gotten the idea the day Natalie had barged into his barn.

I follow through on my promises. Natalie's words, in that lilting, slightly husky voice, taunted him as he worked.

Yeah, right. Forty-eight hours and she hadn't been back. He tossed the piece of incorrectly cut glass into the box that held rejects. Those could be recycled and used another time. The pile had grown since yesterday, but he could use them in a future glass sculpture. Yeah, that was putting a good spin on the situation. He barely knew this woman and her absence for two days didn't give him the right to mope.

I'm a champion of lost causes. A regular St. Jude.

Maybe he was one lost cause too many. Maybe Natalie saw the same thing in him that his mother did so that no matter what he'd accomplished, it wasn't enough. It would never be enough because he wasn't his half brother. Though he and Patrick shared the same mother, they had different fathers. He chose another piece of glass, determined to get this one right. His muse had returned and he wasn't going to let a couple of mistakes stop him. He'd—

A car door slammed in the distance. He started to rise from the stool he'd been perched on but forced himself to sit back down. *What is wrong with you, Gal-*

lagher? He ground his back teeth, but deep down he enjoyed sparring with Natalie, enjoyed being the kind of guy who could attract a wholesome single mother, even if that was temporarily. Even if it was because she wanted something from him.

"Hello? Lieutenant?"

His heart thudded at the sound of her voice and he scowled, angered by his reaction. Making a fool of himself was not on today's agenda.

She appeared around the corner, her straight, blond hair billowing out behind her as if she were a model at a photo shoot. Once again she carried a tin in one hand and had a tight grip on Sam's hand with the other. The boy's bright blue eyes danced above ruddy cheeks as he held up a fistful of colorful candy canes and grinned. Des shifted in his seat and his throat clogged up with emotions at the sight of Natalie and her winsome son.

"Boy, it's windy today. Don't you think so?" she asked but didn't wait for an answer before rushing on. "Sorry we're late but we stopped at the store and well, you know how Tavie is. Talked our ears off, didn't she, Sam? Anyway, that's why we're so late today. Have you wondered where we were?"

Only for two freaking days. "No."

She stepped farther into the barn. "Sam's pediatric neurologist wanted a colleague to exam him, so we drove to Montpelier."

"What's there to do for two days in the state capital?" Damn. He hadn't meant to ask that and he detested the thread of need evident in his voice. What was that about not making a fool of himself?

"You'd be surprised at how much there is to do."

She gave him a blinding smile. "Maybe you should check it out."

"Humph."

"Grumpy again today? Maybe these will help." She set the tin on the bench. "I made you my special home-made minty shortbread cookies dipped in chocolate and topped with sprinkles. Sam put the Christmas sprinkles on them, didn't you, Sam?"

The boy grinned and nodded his head and Des bit back the snark that threatened to roll off his tongue. It wasn't Sam's fault he was such a dumbass around the boy's mother.

"Huh, maybe I should've asked if you liked mint before I inundated you with it, but I see you ate all the bark, so I guess that answers that."

She opened the tin and the scents of peppermint and chocolate wafted out. The green cookies were partially coated with chocolate and red, white and green sprinkles on top of that. They looked delicious, but Des scowled at them, refusing to be coaxed out of his mood by her or her baked goods.

"Problem?" Her gaze flicked between him and the cookies.

He fisted his hands to keep from reaching out and caressing her cute little frown. Or better yet, running his tongue over those furrows in her forehead. He swallowed a groan. "If I keep eating what you bring, I'm going to end up as a carnival sideshow."

She broke into a wide, candid smile, transforming her from attractive to unforgettable. "Didn't you get the memo? Calories don't count in December."

He grumbled but grabbed a cookie and took a bite,

closing his eyes as butter, mint and chocolate exploded in his mouth. These were the best yet. No doubt left, he was a goner.

Natalie gave him an expectant gaze. "What do you think?"

That I've died and gone to heaven. He shrugged. "They're pretty good."

"So…" She met his gaze. "Have you given any thought to making ornaments?"

"Yeah," he said and winced at the hopeful expression on her face. "The answer's still no, but—" he held up the half-eaten cookie "—I applaud your effort."

"Ah, you have a sweet tooth." She gave him a smile that had him wishing he was the kind of man she deserved. "Good to know."

"You can bring a whole bakery and the answer would still be no," he warned and grabbed another cookie. He did not need her getting under his skin any further. The fact that he'd been looking for her for the past two days rankled. And she never quite answered why she'd been gone that long. How many appointments did Sam have? *Yo, Gallagher, none of your business.* So why was he fixating on it? She didn't owe him an explanation, just as he didn't owe her one for refusing to make Christmas-themed glass art pieces.

"But don't you enjoy the feeling you get from doing a good deed?"

Give the lady points for tenacity. He shook his head. "It might alter people's expectations of me."

Instead of being cowed or annoyed by his surly attitude she seemed buoyed, ready to take on the challenge he represented. Des admired that. Yeah, admiration was a nice safe name for what he felt for Natalie Pierce.

"I must say, you're quite the conundrum."

"Really? I've always considered myself more of an enigma." He handed a cookie to Sam and winked. Sam grinned and bit the treat in half.

"Tell you what," Des said and popped the rest of the shortbread into his mouth, but it lost its appeal when her expression turned hopeful again. He was going to disappoint her, but he should be used to disappointing the women in his life. Not that she was *in* his life. Nope. He didn't do charming. Why did he always forget that around her? "I'll make a cash donation to this auction of yours."

"Thank you. And don't think I don't appreciate it, but we would have more earning potential if you made ornaments. More people would attend if we were able to advertise that we'd have your exclusive crafts. Ones that you can't get anywhere else. I don't want to seem ungrateful, but more people would be bidding on them and that would drive up the price."

"I thought it was a silent auction." He tilted his head and raised his eyebrows in a "gotcha" gesture.

Natalie stabbed her finger at him. "Okay, you got me there, but when people see all the bids piling up for your ornaments, they'd bid higher."

"Are you sure you're not overestimating my appeal?"

She blushed. "I don't think that's even possible."

His stupid heart did not stutter. What was he, fifteen? He cleared his throat. "You know I was referring to my art."

She gave him a wide-eyed, innocent expression, but

those baby blues shone with amusement. "Of course. That's what my answer was based on. What did *you* think I meant?"

Sam tugged on her sleeve and she glanced down. "You're right. It's getting late." She glanced up and met Des's gaze. "He has another hippotherapy session today."

He might not do charming, but he admired the heck out of the strong bond she had with Sam. "I wouldn't want him to miss that."

"Especially if it means getting rid of us, *hmm*?"

He held up his hands. Hey, even his jerkiness had its limits. "Honestly, I didn't mean it that way. You said he enjoyed the sessions."

"I was teasing," she said and laid her hand on his arm.

Incapable of speech, Des couldn't think of anything except that she was touching him. The warmth of her hand penetrating the flannel of his shirt had muddled his brain.

"Contrary to the popular consensus, I believe you have a lot buried under all that grumpiness, including a sense of humor." She squeezed his arm before letting her hand drop.

As reason returned and he became capable of speech once again, he lifted a finger and wagged it. "See? That's where you'd be wrong. I'm grumpy on the outside, morose and malcontented on the inside. Unlike you, I don't do optimism."

"Oh, my, you say *optimism* like it's a communicable disease." Her eyes sparkled. "And maybe I choose to see more in you."

He snorted a laugh. Damn, too bad he didn't do cute. Except that argument died a little more each time he saw her and soon that feeble excuse would be on life support. He shook his head and tried to arrange his face in a scowl, but for once those muscles refused to cooperate. His grin snapped back like a rubber band. "Then I seriously question your choices, Ms. Pierce."

"Question them all you want, but it won't change my opinion." Sam tugged on her sleeve again and she nodded to him. "I'll be seeing you soon."

He quirked an eyebrow. "Making threats again?"

She exited the barn, leaving behind her subtle lavender scent and the echo of her laughter. What would it be like to be in her orbit? To know her so well that silent communication was possible?

Des sighed and cut the piece again. This time the curve was perfect. "Coincidence," he muttered as he put the glass in place to create a loon rising from a lake. He believed in a lot of things but coincidence wasn't one of them. Which meant he was in a whole heap of trouble.

Standing, he stretched his back and took a sip of coffee from the insulated mug as he eyed the tin of cookies. He was going to have to add time to his workout regime if he kept this up much longer. He reached for another cookie.

"Umm… Des?"

His head snapped up to find Natalie and Sam still standing in the doorway of the barn. The smile that had started at the sight of her slipped when Sam sniffled as if he'd been crying. Des jumped up and nearly tripped when his leg protested.

"What's wrong? What happened? Is Sam okay?" His

heart pounding, he ignored the pain in his leg to get to them. "Did he get hurt?"

"He's okay… I'm okay…we're both fine." She waved her hand. "I didn't mean to alarm you. It's my car. It won't start. I could call Ogle Whatley's garage, but Sam's session would be over by the time Ogle came out here and fixed it."

Des exhaled, but his heart was still pounding. "Is that why he's crying? He doesn't want to miss his session?"

"I'm sorry. We didn't mean to frighten you." She appeared as distraught as her son. "I'm sure it must seem silly to you but—"

"It's not silly when you're five, is it, Sam?" He held out his hand to the boy. "Want to help me look for the jumper cables? I have some in my truck. If it's your battery, it won't take long to get you going. C'mon, Sam, let's go take a look."

He should resent having his work interrupted now that his muse was back, but the fact was, the sight of either one of them in distress made him want to help. And when Sam slipped his hand in his, Des had the urge to start whistling some stupid, sappy tune.

Natalie hung back as Des and Sam left the barn. She'd thought Des might be put out at having to help her, but he seemed strangely happy. *Don't read too much into it*, she cautioned herself. Maybe he didn't want to upset Sam. As gruff as Des tried to project, he'd been nothing but kind to Sam.

She followed them outside to where Des was pulling jumper cables from a locker in the bed of his pickup.

Sam was standing on his toes, trying to see. "Sam, please don't get in the lieutenant's way."

"Why don't you get back in the car?" she suggested. Sam frowned and she added, "You can watch him from your seat. I'll lower your window."

"I think your mom has a good idea, bud. You might even get a better view than standing on tiptoe," Des said.

After she made sure Sam was buckled into his car seat, she got in the driver's seat and lowered her window. Like son, like mother? She shook her head, but couldn't help gawking as Des leaned over the hood of her Camry to hook the jumper cables to her dead battery. To prevent drooling, she ordered herself to think about the cost of a new battery—and at Christmastime—instead of how luscious his butt looked, caressed by all that faded denim. But it wasn't just his glutes making her mouth water. The stubble that peppered his face, the two-haircuts-past-due thick, black hair and the intense dark brown eyes all sent her pulse racing.

"Natalie?" Des asked, his tone laced with impatience.

Nothing like getting caught daydreaming about the super-hot naval officer. How many times had he called her name? "Sorry. What?"

"I'm going to start my engine and I'll let you know when to try yours again. Wait for my signal."

She nodded and he went to his truck. Once they got her car started, he came back and removed the cables, rolling them up as he walked toward his pickup. She was glad to see that his limp wasn't as pronounced today.

Grabbing the roll of paper towels she had on the passenger seat, Natalie tore off a few. He came back to her car, and she offered him the towels through her open window.

"Thanks." He wiped his hands. "Stay here while I shut the barn door."

"Why?" She checked her watch. Sam's session would be starting soon. "What are you doing?"

"I'm going to follow you and make sure you make it to the therapy place." He spoke as if his actions were a given.

His concern brought delicious warmth to her insides. Again making her yearn for something she hadn't even realized was missing from her current existence. Okay, maybe she'd realized it, but she'd been ignoring the vague discontent. *There's nothing missing. You have a full, satisfying life*, she repeated to herself. And she did. So what if she hadn't dated in the three years since Ryan's death? Sam had been her top priority during that time. Ryan's generous life insurance payout gave her financial stability and the nursery school in Nashville where she'd been employed part-time had permitted Sam to attend free of charge. Here in Loon Lake she'd met Mary Wilson through volunteering at the weekly payment-optional luncheons at the church. When the Wilsons' summer camp cook had taken ill, she'd stepped in. The Wilsons had also allowed her to bring Sam and even invited her back next summer.

Full life or not, since meeting Des she'd wondered if she had room for more. Something more. Or rather, some*one* more. And that was disconcerting.

She stuck her head out the car window. "I'm sure we'll be fine. I've already taken up too much of your time."

He shook his head, his dark hair falling across his forehead. "Unless you plan on letting the car run the entire time you're there, you might need another jump."

She fought the urge to brush his hair back, to touch it to see if it felt as soft as it looked. "That wouldn't be good for the environment, would it?"

"No, ma'am, it wouldn't."

She snickered at his use of *ma'am*. "Aha, I see what you did there."

"So it's settled. I'll follow you."

She'd love for him to come along, but she didn't want him to see her and Sam as a nuisance. Yeah, as if he didn't already, considering the way she'd barged into his life with her demands for Christmas ornaments.

He crossed his arms over his chest. "Besides, aren't you the one trying to convince me to support this enterprise?"

That did make sense. "Are you saying you might be so overcome by what you see, you'll do whatever I ask?"

Des dropped his arms and snorted a laugh. "Too late for that."

A flush of warmth spread through her and she couldn't contain her grin. Was he saying he felt an attraction, too? Was that a possibility? Des might act all gruff and surly but she suspected beneath all that he was a caring man bent on protecting himself. *Don't go spinning fairy tales*, she cautioned herself. Des might be a case of WYSIWYG—What You See is What You Get. Yeah, the problem with rainbow optimism was that you often got your heart broken.

On her wedding day, she'd assumed they'd happily grow old together, but two years later a stranger's careless actions had taken Ryan from them and changed the course of their lives in an instant. Because of it, Sam would have to grow up without his dad.

Ryan had convinced her to drop out of college when Sam was born. He'd had a decent paying job at a tech start-up in Nashville so her degree hadn't been a priority then. Now she understood how short-sighted she'd been.

As much as she needed optimism, facing reality was key to planning for the future.

She waited for Des to come back and climb into his truck before she put the car in gear and made her way to the therapy center.

Conflicting thoughts vied for space in her head during the drive to the stable. She hardly knew Des. Or what had happened to make him keep the world at arm's length. Few wounds healed without permanent scars. She'd have to be crazy to even try bringing him out of his self-imposed exile. She had enough on her plate with Sam, finishing her degree and starting a career, as opposed to the lower-paying jobs she'd had since Ryan's death.

Last year, she'd inherited her grandmother's summer home, a duplex in Loon Lake. After careful deliberation, Natalie had decided not to sell the place, but to move to the quaint town she'd remembered and loved from childhood visits.

Thanks to the inheritance she lived mortgage-free plus collected rent from the tenant on the other side of the two-family home. That monthly rent paid her utility bills and helped with upkeep. With Ryan's generous life insurance payout, she'd been able to spend time with Sam when he'd needed her during his recovery and rehabilitation. But now was the time for a concrete plan for their future. Finishing her degree so she could get a decent job was the first step. She'd set aside a portion of the life insurance for Sam's college fund and had refused to draw from it. Next year, when Sam started school, she'd have more time to devote to online studies or attend classes at the nearest university.

She pulled into the packed earth parking lot of the hippotherapy center and chose two spots together in case Des needed to jump-start her car again. She smiled. It was nice to think someone had her back. Even though she'd lived in Loon Lake for a short time, many of the residents remembered her grandmother and were friendly and helpful, treating her as if she'd lived there all her life. But it would be nice to know she had someone more permanent to share life's ups and downs with. What was she doing? She barely knew this man, so no more spinning fairy tales.

Once the auction benefitting the equine therapy center was over, maybe she could still take baked goods to Des. *And maybe he'd have to take out a restraining order on me.* She laughed at herself as she turned off her engine and got out and opened the rear door. Sam scrambled out of the car and she held out her hand. He dutifully took it, but she knew the day was coming when he'd refuse to comply. She'd gotten into the habit of insisting on holding his hand because he couldn't answer if she called to him.

He'd gotten away from her once when he darted under a rack of clothes in a department store. She'd frantically called to him, despite knowing he couldn't answer. After five agonizing minutes that felt like fifty, she'd found him, but from that day forward she'd insisted he hold her hand in public. She suspected that his seeing her anguished tears that day had scared him and he hadn't fought holding her hand since then.

Turning to Des, who'd parked and was getting out of his truck, she said, "I'm going to take Sam in to get saddled up. Over there by the fence is the perfect spot to watch his session."

He nodded and she took off toward the barn with Sam.

Des leaned against the fence and studied the dirt arena where the sessions were held. He'd used his laptop the second day Natalie had visited to look up information about how hippotherapy worked. At the time he'd justified learning more about it because he'd planned to give Natalie a cash donation for her auction. It had nothing to do with wanting to learn more about the woman who'd barged into his life with an endless supply of chatter and baked goods. But it wasn't the sweets that had invaded his dreams every night. She and her crooked-toothed smile, her big blue eyes and that sweet voice had kept him company the past few nights.

He caught movement in his peripheral vision and turned as Natalie made her way over to him. His heart kicked as it always did when he saw her, but her face lacked its usual sunny expression. The sight of her distress was like a blow to the chest with a two-by-four.

He wanted to reach out but forced himself to stand still, keeping his arms along the fence to keep from pulling her into his arms and crushing her against him. "What's wrong?"

She heaved a sigh. "I found out the program's financial situation is worse than I thought. The owner is close to being evicted from this place."

"If they lose the lease, what will happen to the horses?" he asked, her unhappiness weighing on him.

"I don't know. But without the horses, getting the lease paid up-to-date or getting the business on sound financial footing won't matter. This place relies a lot on volunteers, but there are two part-time employees, in addition to the owners, who would be affected. I'd hate for anyone to lose their job. Not to mention, the nearest therapy center is three hours away." Her bottom teeth scraped her upper lip in what appeared to be a nervous habit. "Driving that far for twice-weekly sessions would be out of the question."

He shoved aside his urge to soothe that lip with his tongue. He needed to concentrate on practical matters, like finding out what sort of business operation was Natalie getting involved in? "How did this place get into such a financial bind to begin with?"

She gave him a sharp look. Yeah, his tone had been gruffer than he'd planned, but he didn't want her getting hurt. Financial or otherwise.

"From what I understand, the owners are going through a contentious divorce," she said.

"So raising money might not even help?" His instinct was to interfere in order to safeguard Natalie and Sam. But he had no right to feel the protective feelings that rose up. They'd known one another a short time. They weren't even friends, just acquaintances.

"I had hoped raising funds would keep the horses safe and in place until something better could be figured out." She waved at Sam, who was smiling proudly as he sat on his horse.

Sam looked at ease atop a seal-brown gelding with one white rear leg. Des considered Sam a sunny, happy child, and he could see how much pleasure he got from riding the horse.

Des cleared his throat. Did he want to bring this up? It was none of his business, but he'd be damned if he stood by and let her be harmed in any way. "You haven't done anything other than organize this auction, have you?"

Her head snapped back and she narrowed her eyes. "What do you mean?"

"I'm talking about infusing this place with cash...as in, your own cash." He curled his hands into fists on top of the cross posts for the fence, waiting for her answer.

She shook her head and raised a hand. "I would never ever do anything to jeopardize Sam's future by putting money into a failing enterprise. And I don't appreciate the inference that I would."

He took her hands in his and winced at how cold they were. He rubbed them to try to warm them up. "I'm not accusing you of anything, Natalie. I wanted to understand what we're dealing with."

"Thanks. I've had a lot of support from family and friends ever since the accident, but sometimes, late at night when I'm alone, I second-guess all my decisions." She grimaced. "I didn't mean to snap, but sometimes guilt—warranted or not—makes me a bit defensive."

He squeezed her hands. "I was worried about you pouring your own cash into a dying business."

"No chance of that." She shook her head and visibly relaxed. "I've been extremely frugal with our finances. I take my obligation to Sam seriously. I want him to be happy, but not to the point where I might jeopardize his future. I'm the parent and need to make the hard decisions."

He let go of her hands. He barely knew Natalie so his relief at her answer was disproportionate to the situation. If she wanted to go bankrupt supporting a failing business that was her problem, but he admired her fierce protectiveness toward her son. As a kid, he would've given anything to have had a mother like Natalie. Heck, he would've been thankful for one who'd taken any interest at all. He cleared his throat. "What if nothing can be figured out?"

She frowned. "Are you always such a pessimist?"

"I'm a realist. I would think you'd be one, too." He regretted the words as soon as they were out of his mouth. "Look, Natalie, I—"

"No, you're probably right." She turned to face the dirt track and Sam. "But I can't think that way. I have to choose optimism. If that's rainbows and unicorns, then so be it."

When he didn't respond, she brought her gaze back to him. "No comeback about my choices?"

He gave in to his urge, running his fingers across her cheek and tucking strands of silky hair behind her ear. "No glib comebacks. Sam's one lucky guy to have you for his mother. Not all mothers practice the kind of unconditional love you have."

"I like to think I'm the lucky one." She smiled at Sam before turning her gaze back to Des. "So you believe not all mothers practice unconditional love? What makes you believe that?"

"I know they don't," he said, thinking of his own. He'd always known Patrick was the golden child but it wasn't until after his brother's death that—

She cupped her hand around his cheek. He should pull away because it wasn't just her mothering he admired. How could she be offering comfort after his callous remark? What kind of woman did that? He leaned into her touch. What would it be like to pull her into his arms, let her warmth sink into those cold places inside him?

She started to pull her hand away, but he reached up and captured it in his. "I apologize for my comment. I may be an insensitive jerk but normally I practice my antisocial tendencies when I'm alone and especially not when I'm in the company of a beautiful woman."

"Apology accepted." She blushed. "After his session, Sam and I always go to the café in town. I hope you'll join us. I want to thank you for getting my car started."

"You should go straight to the garage and have Ogle check the battery. Your old one may not even have kept the charge."

"You're right," she said and frowned. "I know I should've gone straight to Ogle's but…" She turned her head to watch Sam, a tender expression on her pretty face.

He studied her profile as Sam and his horse continued to be led around the ring. Sam grinned and waved to them each time he passed. Des waved, but his attention was on the woman beside him.

"I see how much he enjoys riding," he said.

"He's calmer since he's started spending time with

the horses." Her voice sounded resigned. "We've had our ups and downs. He gets frustrated and can be quick to anger but being around the horses soothes him."

He reached for her hand again. "And what soothes you?"

"Me?" She stared at him, surprised. "I don't think anyone has ever asked me that."

"Maybe they should." He touched her cheek with his other hand. "So tell me what you find soothing."

She looked off in the distance as if trying to decide how to answer.

"I bet I know." His hand moved from her cheek to her hair, unable to resist touching the corn-silk strands.

"Oh? What do you think it is?" she asked, sounding a little breathless.

He contemplated, stalling for time. Then something occurred to him. "Baking. I'll bet baking soothes you."

She seemed to be thinking it over, her gaze meeting his. "I believe you're right, but how did you know?"

He cleared his throat and broke eye contact, glancing at Sam on the horse. "I can taste it."

Before she could say anything, he pointed to Sam, whose horse was being led back into the building. "Looks like he's finished."

To his relief, her focus shifted back to her son. He was not about to admit his feelings about her baking.

After his session, Sam came out from the building and carefully made his way toward them. His gait was slightly stiff, but a huge grin split his face.

"You looked like a jockey up there on that horse, bud," Des told him and held out his hand, palm up. The kid slapped it and although it seemed impossible, Sam's smile got even bigger. What was it about this boy and his mother that called to Des?

"You did great, Sam, but I'm afraid I have some bad news for you. We won't be able to go to the café like I promised. I need to take the car to Ogle's garage for a new battery. We can get some snacks at Tavie's store while we wait if you're hungry."

Even though the Loon Lake General Store was next door to Ogle's garage, Des didn't think a few packaged snacks were as much fun as going to Aunt Polly's Café. And he was right; the boy's face fell. "You like Polly's pancakes, don't you?"

Sam grinned up at him and nodded his head vigorously.

Natalie's eyes widened. "How did you know that's what he always orders?"

"Because having pancakes when it's not breakfast is fun, right, Sam?"

Again, the boy grinned and nodded. Des answered with a wink.

Natalie put her hand on Sam's shoulder. "I'm not sure how long it will take for the battery to be replaced, if that's even what's wrong. The café is only open for breakfast and lunch, but we'll try."

Des cleared his throat. "I have an idea. I'll follow you to the garage and we'll go to Aunt Polly's while Ogle is checking out your car." What was he doing? Did he suggest they go to eat? As in *together*? As in a public place? Not only would he be seen in public, but also with a woman *and* her son. Gossip would be flying from one end of town to the other.

She turned to Des, her eyes wide. "Are you sure you don't mind?"

No, he wasn't sure, but he wasn't about to change his mind and disappoint Sam. But it wasn't just about Sam, was it? He wanted to spend time with Natalie, plain and simple. But could he do that without falling under her spell? And he had no doubts this woman could cast a spell. So he'd take them to lunch, make a donation to her charity and that would be the end of it. He could handle that, right? It wasn't as if he was getting involved with her or anything. She'd have her car fixed, Sam would have his pancakes and afterward Des would go back home and things would return to normal. "I don't mind. Let's go and see if your car will start."

Her car did need another jump. Good thing he'd insisted on coming with her. In a town like Loon Lake she wouldn't have been stranded for long, but he didn't like the idea of her stranded at all. Yeah, because he was a regular Dudley Do Right. His sudden altruism had nothing to do with his burgeoning feelings for Natalie... right?

Chapter Three

As soon as Des walked into the café with Natalie and Sam, he knew he'd made a grave tactical error. The other customers did a double take at the sight of the three of them together. Natalie was popular and well-liked because everyone smiled and waved or nodded to her. He could see the reputation he'd cultivated as someone unapproachable crumbling before his eyes.

A short, blond waitress pointed to a booth. "Be right with you folks."

Once they were seated, Natalie pulled a small packet of crayons out of her purse along with a pad of paper and handed them to Sam. Reaching back into the voluminous bag, she set a miniature car next to the pad. Sam began drawing a picture of the toy.

She glanced up and caught Des watching her. "What?"

"Just wondering what else you have in there." Des hitched his chin toward her humongous bag.

Wiggling her eyebrows, she grinned. "Wouldn't you like to know."

He shook his head and chuckled. "That's one challenge I'm not crazy enough to take on. I know that a woman's purse is sacrosanct. You do not touch without permission."

Amusement flickered in her eyes. "Someone taught you well."

"Any woman I've ever known has always said 'get my purse' instead of 'look in my purse.'"

She laughed. "Yeah. I guess you're right."

"Of course I am. Don't you agree, Sam?"

Sam looked at him, then his mom. When he turned back, his expression said he knew better than to get involved. Des couldn't hide his grin.

Her gaze bounced around the restaurant. "Do you have any idea why everyone is staring at us? Sam and I come here every week and that's never happened before."

He shrugged. "I can't say for sure, but I'll bet it's because you're with me."

"Oh." She swallowed. "So you're…like more famous than I thought."

He bit back his laugh and shook his head. "*Infamous* is more like it. I bet they're all wondering what the heck a nice girl like you is doing with someone like me."

"Now, why would they be thinking that?" she asked, her face suffused with color.

Des loved seeing that flush, knowing he'd put it there. If he wasn't careful, he'd be getting in deeper than he intended. But when she looked at him like that, he found it impossible to stop teasing.

He shrugged. "You said it yourself. I cloak myself in grumpiness like it's a virtue."

She blushed again. "I shouldn't have said that. I apologize."

"Why? Have you changed your mind about my behavior?"

"No, but I've changed my mind about calling you out on it." She gave him an impish smile that once again melted his resolve. "My mother would be appalled at my being so openly rude."

He quirked an eyebrow. "But it's acceptable if you hide it?"

"My mother definitely would have preceded any insult with 'bless your heart,' Lieutenant."

"And that would mean?"

"That you couldn't help your behavior." She leaned across the table. "Bless your heart. I just love how you don't care what people think."

He barked a laugh and swore that a hushed silence descended on the whole place as if everyone else was holding their breath. Damn, he was ruining his reputation.

The waitress who'd pointed them to the booth appeared with a tray containing two ruby-red pebbled plastic tumblers filled with water. She also had a white disposable cup with a cover and a straw, which she handed to Sam. "Hey, little man, welcome back. And I see you've brought a new friend with you today. I often wondered what it would take to get our resident hermit into town." She set the glasses on the table. "What did you two have to threaten him with to get him here? As far as I know, he'd never come here willingly. And smiling about it, too."

Des rolled his eyes and shook his head, but winked when Sam caught him.

"Hi, Trudi," Natalie greeted the waitress. "Most people don't know this about me, but I was a lion tamer before I had Sam."

Trudi held the empty tray across her chest and looked Des up and down. "Nah. This one is more grizzly than lion, if you ask me."

"Then maybe it's a good thing no one is asking you," Des said. Being with Natalie and Sam may have stunted his gruffness, but he couldn't let Trudi's comment pass without a response.

Trudi blew out her breath and grinned. "Is he always this entertaining?"

Natalie gave him a smile that increased his heart rate, then said, "I wouldn't be here with him if he wasn't."

If he wasn't careful he'd start grinning like a lovesick idiot. How the heck had she gotten him to do any of this? He glanced across the booth at Natalie and scowled. If he wasn't careful, he might start thinking he could still have the happy ending he'd dreamed about once upon a time.

Natalie shifted in her seat in the café across from Des, who was scowling at her. He seemed to do that every time she thought she'd drawn him out of his grumpy self. Was he angry with her for the quips with the waitress? No, he had a sharp sense of humor buried under all the surliness. Maybe that scowl was a defense mechanism like her fake smile when people commented on Sam's lack of verbal skills.

"Is Sam wanting his usual?" Trudi asked into the sudden silence. She stood poised to take their orders, pencil in one hand, pad in the other.

Sam frowned and pointed at Des, who looked to her with a helpless expression and Natalie had to clear the sudden clog in her throat.

"I think he wants you to order first." She'd grown accustomed to deciphering Sam's wants and needs, but Des seemed lost. She wanted a male role model in Sam's life, but she needed one that wouldn't simply be passing through. She needed to be careful Sam didn't get his heart broken. She made a mental note to see if Loon Lake had any sort of a Big Brother program.

"What's Sam's usual?" Des asked the waitress.

"Malted pancakes with warm maple syrup and a dollop of whipped cream on top," Trudi said.

Des turned to Sam. "You recommend that?"

Sam gave him a thumbs-up.

"Sounds perfect. I'll have that." Des handed the menu back to the waitress and nodded to Sam. "You have good taste."

Relieved by the easy exchange between Des and Sam, Natalie laughed as she handed the menus back. "What the heck, it's the holidays. Make it three."

"I have it on good authority that calories don't count in December," Des said after the waitress had scurried away.

"So my chatter isn't all background buzz for you. Good to know." She was teasing, but on some deeper level she was serious. Not that she'd ever admit it to him. Nor did she want to admit that she cared about what he thought.

He grunted. "You do tend to talk a lot." He glanced at Sam, then met her gaze. "But I guess it's understandable."

She swallowed against the sudden burn in the back of her eyes. Reaching over, she took a sip of water to collect her thoughts before speaking. "We've been practicing communicating with his iPad, haven't we, Sam?"

Sam scrunched his nose and shook his head before going back to his crayons and paper. Natalie looked out the window at the Christmas wreaths hanging from the lampposts lining Main Street. She loved how the town exuded Christmas spirit and in times like this she was glad she'd moved to Loon Lake to raise Sam. Even if living here meant driving an hour or two for appointments with specialists in pediatric neurology. But in the end, what if she'd been wrong to move away from all that Nashville had to offer Sam? Was she doing right by her child? Or simply doing what she wanted?

A warm, callused hand squeezed hers and interrupted her brooding. She lifted her head and her gaze collided with deep brown eyes.

"Recovery's not always a straight line. It doesn't mean you've done anything wrong," Des said softly.

It was as if he'd read her mind, recognized her self-doubt. Was that one of the many reasons she was drawn to him? Did it have to do with his hiding pain the way she did? She knew all about that. Natalie had meant it when she said she chose to be cheerful and optimistic, but that didn't mean that she didn't have her doubts when she was trying to fall asleep at night.

Des chose to mask his pain behind a gruff exterior. She didn't know what had happened to him but she suspected his limp had to do with the end of his naval career. Why had she never asked him? Scolding herself for being so selfish, she said, "Thank you. I—"

"And here we go, malted pancakes with whipped cream." Trudi stopped at the end of the booth with her tray. The plates were piled high with pancakes topped with mounds of whipped cream.

Des removed his hand from hers, but Natalie knew his gesture had piqued Trudi's interest. Yup, she and Des would be the next hot topic of conversation and endless speculation. She may not have been in Loon Lake long, but she knew how small-town gossip worked.

Trudi set the tray down and passed out the plates before putting a clear glass syrup dispenser in the middle of the table. "And warm maple syrup. The best part, right, Sam? If you need anything else, let me know." The waitress wiped her hands on her apron. "And if Sam here needs a refill on these pancakes, it's on the house."

"You've got a sweet deal here, Sam," Des said and gave him a thumbs-up.

Sam grinned. Natalie's stomach fluttered and she mouthed "thank you" to Des over Sam's head as he bent over his plate to dig into his pancakes. His questioning expression told her he wasn't sure why she was thanking him. But then, neither was she. Perhaps it was that she appreciated the way he treated Sam. Or could it be the way he treated *her*?

She and Des talked about the hippotherapy center and the horses while they ate. Des did his best to include Sam by asking direct questions that her son could answer with a nod or shake of the head. By the time they'd finished the pancakes, her admiration of Des Gallagher had increased twofold. And not just because of the way he treated Sam. She wasn't so naive as to think her feelings only had to do with her son.

Trudi came back to the table and asked Sam if he needed more, but he shook his head and patted his stomach.

"You folks will need to walk off all those calories. You three might want to go across the square to Libby Taylor's quilt and craft shop," Trudi said as she collected their empty plates and stacked them, piling the utensils on top with a *cling-clang.* "I hear Libby's setting up one of those miniature Christmas villages in the front window complete with a train." She juggled the dirty plates against her chest and slapped the bill facedown on the table. "I'll bet Sam will love the train."

Sam's eyes widened and he looked toward Des. Sam didn't have to say anything because the pleading look on his face said it all.

Natalie's scalp prickled at the thought of Sam looking to Des for permission after having her son to herself for three years. Of course she didn't want to limit Sam's world, but neither did she want him to get his heart broken. She couldn't protect him from all of life's hurts, but as a mother she had to at least try.

"It's up to your mom," Des said in a neutral tone.

She tried to gauge how Des felt about going to see the window display. He'd made it pretty clear how much he disliked Christmas.

"You're probably champing at the bit to get back

home. If you don't want to go, I can bring him some other time," she said, giving Des an out if he wanted one.

His brow furrowed as he seemed to be thinking it over. "What I have waiting at home will still be there tomorrow. We'll settle up here and head on over before we go to pick up your car. How's that sound to you, Sam?"

Sam looked as though he was imitating a bobble-head doll.

"Okay." She had a feeling she looked as excited as her son but for different reasons. Nope, it wasn't a ceramic village with a train that she found so appealing but a handsome six-foot-two former navy lieutenant.

She reached for the bill, but Des was faster and scooped it up. "My treat."

"But I invited you so I should pay." She held out her hand.

He gave her his usual scowl and held the bill close to his chest. "When I go to a restaurant with a woman, I like to pay."

"You're not going turn out to be some sort of misogynist, are you?"

He grinned. "Nah, just old-fashioned."

Impulsively, she reached over and brushed her hand across his arm. It wasn't skin-to-skin contact but it proved as powerful to her psyche. "In that case, Sam and I thank you, don't we, Sam?"

As Des paid, she made sure Sam's jacket was zipped up and cautioned him to put his mittens on. Her son gave a long-suffering sigh but put them on.

"They were talking about snow by the end of the week," she remarked as the three of them left the restaurant.

"Glad someone is excited for it." Des chuckled as he zipped up his distressed leather bomber jacket.

She gripped Sam's hand as they crossed the street, but let go when they reached the paved path that led through the town green. He ran a little ahead of them. She and Des strolled side by side along the walkway that meandered through the park. Birds chirped in the pine and aspen trees and squirrels darted about, gathering food as if they'd all listened to the same weather forecast predicting snow.

"Does the weather bother your leg?" she asked.

"Only when I walk."

"Oh, dear, then maybe we shouldn't—"

He bumped shoulders with her. "I was joking. Walking is good. Keeps it limber."

"Does it get stiff often?" she asked, her gaze on Sam as he walked ahead, his arm outstretched at a ninety degree angle with the toy car as if it was driving through the green.

Des made a strange sound, a cross between a laugh and a cough, but hadn't answered her question, so she turned toward him. "I was asking if— Oh."

He was rubbing his hand over his mouth, his deep brown eyes full of humor.

She choked back her hoot of embarrassed laughter, not wanting to attract Sam's attention. She gave an exasperated sniff. "You do know I was asking about your leg?"

He nodded, his lips twitching. "Of course. What else could you have meant?"

"I think that sense of humor you do your best to hide has a wide streak of juvenileness running through it."

He bumped his shoulder against hers. "I think juvenile humor attaches itself to the Y chromosome."

"I think you're right." She bumped him back. "Ryan's humor could be juvenile at times."

"Ryan's your late husband?"

Damn. Bringing him up couldn't be a good idea, but she'd started to feel comfortable with Des. "Yeah, but maybe I shouldn't have brought him up. Didn't mean to cast a pall over everything."

He shook his head. "You didn't. He was a part of your life and you shouldn't have to apologize for saying his name."

"Thanks." She sighed. "Next year he will have been gone longer than we were married. What about you? Have you ever been married?"

He stared straight ahead. "Came close once."

"Oh?" She tilted her head to look at him, wanting to know more, and yet, not.

"I dodged a bullet there." He stuck his hands in his jacket. "She seemed to think pilots were interchangeable."

Did he still care for her, mourn the end of their relationship? This mystery woman from his past might have changed *her* mind about marrying Des but that didn't necessarily follow that he had. "I'm sorry."

He gave her a curious look. "Why? You had nothing to do with it."

She chuckled. "Sor— Um, I must warn you, along with all my other shining qualities, I'm a knee-jerk apologist."

"As far as faults go, that is one I could live with," he

said. Then, as if realizing what he'd said, he cleared his throat. "So how did you come to settle in Loon Lake?"

"I inherited a duplex from my grandmother. I remembered visits to Loon Lake from my childhood and decided to come back as an adult before I decided what to do with the home."

"Obviously, you liked what you saw."

She smiled broadly. "I did. Took one look at Main Street and fell in love. After living in so many different places growing up, I felt as though I'd come home. And the people are so friendly and caring. So how did you end up here?"

He scrunched one side of his face and closed one eye. "Because the people are so friendly?"

She burst out laughing and bumped shoulders with him. "Juvenile or not, you have a wonderful sense of humor."

"Glad you think so." He chuckled, then grew serious. "Actually, I met Riley Cooper at Walter Reed and he mentioned he was coming here for R&R, so I decided to check it out."

"I know Riley's wife, Meg. I've volunteered a few times at the weekly luncheon at the church—" she motioned toward the soaring steeple at the end of the town green "—and she mentioned he'd been in the marines before they got married."

"Yeah, he came and basically never left. Got married, started a family and now he's a sheriff's deputy for Loon Lake."

"So you're friends with Riley?" Had Des wanted

with his ex-girlfriend the happy family that Riley now had with Meg?

"Not really. He mentioned Loon Lake and since I didn't have anywhere else to go…" He turned away and kicked a small stone.

Having no ties to anything was sad, but she decided not to call him out and embarrass him. She'd had a rootless childhood, so she knew the feeling of not belonging to any one place, but she'd had her parents to anchor her. They weren't a location but they represented home to her. Perhaps that was why she'd wanted to raise Sam in Loon Lake, give him some deep roots to fall back on. "You couldn't have picked a better place than Loon Lake. And I must say, you have a beautiful home."

"Yeah, I had thought that maybe Ashley would change her mind about a future with me when she saw it."

So the former fiancée had a name. Ashley. And it sounded as if maybe he did want what Riley had. Natalie had a love/hate relationship with a woman she'd never met. She hated her for hurting Des, and yet if she hadn't, he might now be a married man and not sharing this pleasant day with her. "Then it's her loss. Your house is gorgeous." She touched his arm. Sensing his withdrawal, she searched for a lighter tone. "Of course, I haven't been inside. The interior could be hideous."

Her deflection worked, because he chuckled again. "Not hideous. Perhaps a bit sparse. I spend most of my time in the workshop in the barn."

"Have you worked with stained glass for a long time?"

"I was interested in all forms of art before—" He stopped, then cleared his throat. "A long time ago, and did some projects during my recovery and continued to work on them after I left the navy. I kept on when I found out people were willing to pay money for them."

Before what? What had he been about to say? They were reaching the end of the path and Sam was getting close to the road, so she didn't pursue it. "Sam, wait for us."

Des was glad she didn't press him about what he'd been about to say. He never talked about the loss of Patrick. Maybe that was wrong. Maybe he should be more like Natalie, who talked about her late husband.

They'd caught up to Sam, who was waiting on the sidewalk that bordered the town square, and crossed the street together. Sam hadn't even tried to dart into the street, but Des understood that was Natalie's fear. What had happened to Sam must have increased her fears.

Natalie motioned with her hand. "Libby's shop is right down there. The one with the navy blue awning in the middle of the block."

Sam pocketed his toy car and hustled ahead of them toward the shop.

He tipped his head in her direction. "Don't tell me you make quilts as well as all that delicious baking?"

"I'm a woman of many talents." Her teasing smile was dazzling.

Catching his breath, he leaned closer to whisper, "Mmm…tell me more."

She turned to face him and her eyes sparkled with

mischief. "Isn't a woman supposed to preserve some mystery?"

He gave her a mock scowl. "That's the way you're going to play it?"

"I am." She nodded firmly but her lips twitched. "For now."

He shifted so his arm brushed against hers. "That sounds promising."

They reached the shop and Sam had his nose pressed to the window, watching a small train chug along a wooden track.

"He's into trains," she said. "And planes and fire trucks, police cars, race cars. You name it. He's hoping Santa Claus will bring him a big LEGO set, but he can't decide between an airport or a fire station or police station."

Sam tugged on Natalie's sleeve and pointed to Des.

An expression Des couldn't read flitted across her face before she said, "I think he wants to know which one you'd pick."

Des chuckled. "I'd pick the airport for obvious reasons, but they all sound exciting and you should ask for the one you want the most."

Sam seemed to consider this advice, then nodded and went back to watching the train run through the miniature village.

"Were you always interested in flying?" she asked.

"My older brother had the dream first. I guess it rubbed off." He left out the part about how he'd tried and failed to fill Patrick's shoes after his brother's death. Even before then, though, he hadn't measured up in his mother's eyes. And he knew how his biological father felt. Despite the man's lack of interest when he was growing up, Des had still reached out as an adult. But his father had felt responding to his own child wasn't important enough, since it might jeopardize his marriage. He pushed the past away, wanting to enjoy this day with Natalie.

"I'm glad you got to fly, even if it did come to an end." She touched his arm. "You should be proud of what you accomplished."

Huh, maybe she had a point. He'd spent a lot of time thinking about what he'd lost and not enough on what he'd done. A weight near his chest shifted and eased at her admiring tone. "Thanks." And he found he meant it.

He stood close enough so the slightest movement from either one caused them to brush against one another, close enough to breathe in her scent. And close enough to be in her orbit, if only for a short time. He pretended to watch the train chugging along a track, weaving between colorful ceramic houses and businesses, but he was concentrating on Natalie, attuned to her slightest movement.

"Oh, look, Sam," Natalie said and pointed to a poster taped to a lower corner of the plate glass window. "They're going to have a tree-lighting ceremony. Remember that big evergreen we passed in the park near the gazebo? They're going to light it up for Christmas. That sounds like fun."

Sam nodded and looked over to Des. She threw him an apologetic look over Sam's head.

"I think he wants you to come with us," she said.

He was caught off guard and hesitated.

She put her arm around Sam's shoulders. "How about we let the lieutenant think it over? It's not until the weekend."

Sam nodded but kept shooting him furtive glances as they started to walk back toward the green.

"I apologize if Sam put you on the spot by inviting you to the town tree-lighting," she said after they'd crossed the street.

"No problem. I'm flattered that he wanted me to go with you guys."

"Well, you're welcome to come but don't feel bad if you choose not to. There'll be lots of people there that I know."

Did she not want him to go with them? After all, the invitation had come from Sam. But it had come via Natalie. Could she have interpreted Sam's request to coincide with her wants? "Yeah. You've met more people in three months than I've met in three years."

"I'm not the town's hermit," she pointed out with a grin.

"Me? Really?" He'd never cared what the townspeople called him or thought of him...until now.

"Yes, you. I wasn't here before Brody Wilson got married and became a father, but I hear he was a bit of a loner. But he's become an upstanding pillar of the community, now that he and Mary have a family and run summer camps from their farm on the edge of town. So I think the moniker now belongs to you."

"Bah, humbug, he wasn't a true hermit. Before he and Mary even started their summer camps, he had an animal sanctuary on his farm and from what I understand, he used to allow farmers to drop off unwanted animals. Obviously, he was a soft touch." Des had made sure no one did anything like that with him.

"Are you saying you wouldn't let that happen?"

"Exactly."

"Well, his animals are well cared for and his camps are successful. He has programs for foster children and at-risk youth. And now I hear he's planning one for kids with cancer."

"The poor guy." He tsked his tongue but didn't believe it. "You wouldn't catch me opening my place to people or animals."

She scowled at him, but the sparkle in her blue eyes gave her away. "Every time I see him, he's got a big smile on his face."

He chuckled. "I'll bet that smile has more to do with Mary than camps or animals."

"So you believe in true love?"

"Ha! That's about as believable as—" He glanced at Sam, who was still walking ahead of them, and leaned closer. "That guy in the red suit."

She bumped his shoulder. "I hope you're not letting one bad experience sour you on love."

"You can hope all you want, but it won't change my mind."

"Just like with the Christmas ornaments?"

He nodded. "Exactly."

"And I'm still determined not to give up on lost causes."

"In that case, I'll take care not to get lost."

They walked through the town green and back to his truck. He couldn't help wondering what it would be like to have Natalie believe in him. She didn't seem to mind that he couldn't fly fighter jets anymore.

Being with Natalie gave him a calm feeling because he didn't have to justify any of his choices or try to be something he wasn't. She accepted him as he was.

Chapter Four

"Will you be glad to get home?" Natalie glanced in the rearview mirror and smiled when Sam nodded his head. Three days had passed since they'd gone to the café for pancakes with Des and she'd missed talking to him. Once she'd gotten home, she'd received a phone call from her mother-in-law, Bev, whose sister had had a stroke. Natalie had driven to Boston that night so Bev could see her grandchild. This morning they'd taken Bev to the airport; she was going to catch an early flight to Tampa, Florida, to care for her sibling.

Would Des wonder what had happened to them? She hadn't driven to his place to tell him she'd be going out of town. It wasn't as if they had a proper relationship. Did they even share a friendship? Or were they more like acquaintances? She and Sam had been gone three days, but it felt longer. Truth was, she'd missed Des more than she could imagine, and that could become a problem if he didn't feel the same. She still couldn't be sure he wasn't still in love with his ex, Ashley. He'd said he'd come close to getting married. Had they been engaged when she broke up with him?

She had been married before, so she had no right to her jealousy—and yet, there it was. But emotions were not always rational, were they?

Enough thinking about Des Gallagher. For all she knew, he might be celebrating her absence, wondering how he'd gotten so lucky. He'd made it clear he wouldn't become part of the community the way Brody had. But that fleeting expression she'd glimpsed on his face when Sam indicated he wanted Des to join them for the tree-lighting haunted her. She'd recognized yearning in that brief, unguarded moment. She'd recognized it because she was intimately familiar with that particular feeling.

Trying to force her mind onto another topic, she glanced in the rearview mirror at Sam. "I'm sure Shadow will be glad to see you."

They'd adopted a black-and-silver tabby two months ago when the stray had shown up at the hippotherapy center. Sam had fallen in love with the sweet, loving cat the moment he'd laid eyes on it and she hadn't been able to say no. They'd named him Shadow because the kitten followed Sam from room to room as if afraid Sam would disappear if out of sight. Obviously, the cat returned Sam's feelings.

"I'll bet Shadow missed you, but I'm sure Miss Addie and Teddy took good care of him for you."

She pulled into the driveway and parked in the three-sided carport. Sam had unbuckled his seat belt by the time she opened his door. He scrambled out of his booster seat and ran toward the entrance leading to the laundry/mud room, eager to get to his kitten. She followed him to the door and unlocked it. He ran inside to look for Shadow.

She was taking off her jacket in the kitchen when there was a knock at the back door. Natalie smiled when she saw her neighbor through the window in the door and let her in.

"Welcome back," Addie said. Addie Miller had moved into the other side of the duplex with her much younger half brother several months ago. Natalie didn't know the whole story but their mother couldn't take care of Teddy, and Addie had temporary custody. Sam and Teddy had bonded over LEGOs and the boy had accepted Sam and made allowances for his lack of verbal skills.

"Glad to be back." Natalie gave Addie a hug. "Thank you for taking care of the cat."

"Happy to help out. I wanted to let you know what's happened while you were gone." Addie leaned against the kitchen counter. "There's a rumor going around that the horses are gone from the hippotherapy center."

Natalie and Addie had become fast friends as well as neighbors. Natalie had told her all about Sam's therapy sessions and how much he enjoyed the horses.

"Gone? What happened?" Her stomach began to cramp at the news.

"I don't know." Addie shook her head. "I found out about it an hour ago when one of the parents stopped by to see if you knew anything."

"Do you know who could have taken the horses?" Had the owners or creditors auctioned them? Bile rose in her throat. Sam had made such great strides since he'd started the therapy six months ago. His balance issues had almost disappeared. She couldn't be sure if it was all due to the horses or part of the recovery process. But more importantly, he'd bonded with Augie, the dark bay gelding he considered "his" horse.

Addie shrugged. "I'm sorry. I don't. All I know is what that other mother said. Why don't you go and see for yourself? Maybe you can find out something."

Natalie took a deep breath and searched for calm. "Are you sure? I hate to—"

"I understand," Addie interrupted and patted her arm. "Let him stay. Teddy missed him."

"I can't tell you how much it means to me for Sam to have a friend like Teddy." And she meant it. It was good for Sam to interact with boys close to his age.

"I could say the same. Coming here has been an adjustment for Teddy, too. He refuses to talk to me about it, but I fear he's having some trouble fitting in at school. The other kids in his class have been together since kindergarten."

"I'm sorry to hear it. I hate that for Teddy. I hope you can figure out how to get him to open up. I have a feeling Sam will be facing challenges, too."

Addie patted Natalie's shoulder. "We'll be able to form our own support group."

"It's a deal. But for now I've got to see what's going on with the horses. As long as you don't mind keeping Sam." She hated leaving him, but she wouldn't be able to rest until she learned the fate of the whole operation. Yes, she worried about the horses, but also the employees and the children like Sam who depended on the therapy sessions.

"Sam will be fine with me." Addie made a shooing motion with her hands. "Go. Take care of your stuff and don't worry."

"Okay, you have my cell number if you need me." She was convinced and grateful for her friend. It was times like this that she knew she'd made the right choice in moving to Loon Lake.

Natalie drove first to the hippotherapy center, her stomach in her throat the entire way. She wanted to get all the information she could before having to break the news to him. Augie wasn't just Sam's therapy horse; he and the gentle horse were friends. They seemed to have a bond that didn't need words. Good thing, since Sam didn't have any. Why was parenting always one step forward and two steps back?

She inhaled deeply. Enough feeling sorry for herself. That wasn't who she was. She'd get there and find out what was going on and how she could help. Then she'd set about helping. That was what she did, and continued to do, after learning how the TBI had affected Sam.

The first thing she noticed when she pulled up to the center was a for-lease sign. Not a harbinger of good things to come. She parked her car and got out. The place looked deserted. And she couldn't hear the usual activity. Normally at this time of the day, someone would be cleaning out the stalls and feeding the horses.

"Hello?" she called as she approached. Nothing.

She anxiously picked up her phone and called Roberta, one of Sam's therapists.

"Hi, Roberta. I'm at the hippotherapy center, but it's deserted. Do you have any idea what happened?"

"I'm so sorry, Natalie. All I know is the owner called yesterday and asked me to contact my patients and cancel their appointments. You had already told me you were out of town, so I hadn't called you yet. The owner said something about losing the lease."

Her breath hitched. How naive she'd been for believing she could pull off a miracle. "I had no idea things were that bad."

"Believe me, you're not the only one."

"I'm worried about the horses. Do you know where they are?" Her heart pounding, she waited for the other woman's answer.

"I'm sorry but I have no idea."

"Okay. Thanks." She shuddered at the sour taste flooding her mouth.

"Please keep me up-to-date."

"Of course." Natalie ended the call.

Trudging back to her car, she had the overwhelming need to talk to Des. That was crazy; she barely knew him and yet she felt the urge to talk to him. Des Gallagher wasn't a demonstrative man and yet she sought the comfort of his presence. She ignored the voice that accused her of avoiding going home and telling Sam as she headed toward Des's place instead of hers.

If he asked her why she'd come, she could always explain that she might not need his help on the auction after all. She could make up excuses, think up reasons to justify going, but the simple truth was she'd missed him and wanted to see him. It had barely been three full days and she was missing him. Oh, man, she was in trouble. She'd just gotten back in town and here she was racing out to his place.

What if he didn't want to see *her*? What if he was enjoying the peace and quiet without her chatter? And it wasn't as if he could do anything himself about the horses. They were gone. As was her excuse to continue to see Des unless he wanted to see her, too. She pulled into his driveway and parked next to his truck. Leaving her purse on the passenger seat, she got out and went in search of him.

The barn seemed the best bet so she headed there first to look for him. As she approached, noises emanating from the building had her slowing her steps as she listened. It couldn't be what she thought, could it? She quickened her steps. The closer she got, the harder her heart pounded. Were those horses? The echoing whinnies and nicker sounded like it. She inhaled. The air smelled like hay. What was going on?

She entered the barn and stopped dead in her tracks. The hooks on the rough wooden barn walls now held bridles, lead ropes and halters.

Des stood in front of one of the stalls, talking to…a horse? A familiar-looking animal stuck his head over the door.

"I know this is all very confusing to you, but I'm sure Sam and his mom will be stopping by sometime soon. You looking forward to seeing your buddy Sam?" Des rubbed Augie's head. "You've got to eat or you won't have any energy when Sam gets here."

Was she dreaming? She blinked, but Des and Augie were still there. "Des?"

He turned toward her. "You're back."

She took several steps toward him and noticed the color high on his cheeks. She smiled. Looked like the gruff lieutenant was embarrassed to get caught chatting with a horse. "What's going on?"

He looked past her. "Where's Sam?"

"He's with my neighbor. I didn't want to take him with me to an empty hippotherapy center."

Several more horses stuck their heads out of different stalls at the sound of her voice. She counted and all five of the horses from the center were here. *In Des's barn.* Shocked, she rubbed her eyes, but the horses were all still here. What did this mean? Thoughts tumbled over one another in her mind, leaving her disoriented.

She tried to swallow but her mouth was too dry. "Des, what's going on?"

He crossed his arms over his chest. "First, I have a question for you. Where have you been?"

"Boston," she answered automatically. "My mother-in-law—Ryan's mother—needed to fly unexpectedly to Florida. Sam and I wanted to say goodbye since she'll be gone during Christmas. We gave her a ride to the airport." Why was she babbling? "Never mind all of that. I have to know how the horses got here."

"In a livestock trailer. That's the best way to transport—"

"Very funny." She poked him on the shoulder. "Tell me why."

"Hey, in my defense, *how* was your original question." He chuckled and grabbed her hand when she tried to poke him again. "Brody Wilson called and explained, or rather begged, for my help. Seems that Riley Cooper heard that the owner of the center had walked away and abandoned the horses. Riley mentioned it to his wife, Meg, who told Mary, who got Brody involved." He exhaled loudly. "Small-town life in action."

She blinked back tears. "And you brought them here."

He shrugged. "Brody had no room for them at his place. His stalls are all full."

He tilted his head from side to side. "Brody threatened to get Tavie Whatley involved. And I wasn't about to find out if his threats were serious. I know when I've been bested."

"Do you know how to take care of them?" While working at the Wilsons' summer camp, she saw how much care horses required.

"Yeah, I worked on a dude ranch enough summers to know what to do and if I need help or information, there's always Brody for advice."

"I can't tell you how wonderful this is! Desmond Gallagher, you're my hero."

Throwing her arms around him, she pressed her lips to his. She'd intended the kiss as a quick thanks, but when she would have pulled away, his arms went around her. He urged her closer, turning the chaste contact into something more.

He ran the tip of his tongue along the seam of her closed lips and she opened her mouth. This was the kiss she'd been thinking about, dreaming about, longing for, since her second visit. His tongue slipped in and caressed hers as she sighed and gave herself over to the exquisite things his lips and tongue were doing to her. She rejoiced as parts of her, dormant for so long, came alive again.

* * *

Des tightened his hold on her. Kissing Natalie was everything he'd imagined. Literally. But this was better because it was real. She kissed with that same curious mixture of enthusiasm and nervous shyness she'd shown since barging into his barn that first day.

A horse whinnied and she pulled back.

"Umm…uh… I guess I got a little carried away. I—I hope I didn't embarrass you." She smiled but her lips trembled, letting Des know that she wasn't unaffected by what had happened.

Oh, he was embarrassed, too, but not by her or the kiss. It was his reaction to having his lips on hers that was tying him in knots, making him feel like a hormone-pumped teenager.

"No. I think we…uh…we both got caught up in the moment." He cleared his throat. "I'm glad I could help with the horses."

"I don't care what you say, you're my hero for stepping up."

He shook his head. As much as he enjoyed hearing those words from Natalie, he didn't deserve them. His actions didn't come from a place of altruism. Quite the opposite. She thought he was someone he wasn't. That was why he shouldn't get involved with someone like Natalie. She'd always be looking for the good in him. What happened when her search turned up empty? "I'm no hero. For you or anyone."

"To these horses you are. Who knows what might have happened to them if you hadn't rescued them." Joy shone in her eyes.

As much as it pained him, he needed to set her

straight because he liked that look in her eyes, liked it too much. It started giving him ideas for a future he'd put away three years ago. "I didn't rescue them... I'm giving them a place to stay while you sort out what's going to happen with the therapy program as a whole."

"Even so, I appreciate what you did and I know the others who've benefited from the program will, too." Her smile broadened.

He shook his head. "I didn't do it for them."

"What do you mean? Why did you do it?" she asked, confusion evident in her features.

"I did it for you. I knew how concerned you'd been." He sighed and ran his hand through his hair. Maybe he should've left the situation alone. "When Brody called, he sounded desperate. And since this used to be a horse farm..." He shrugged.

At least all the running around he'd had to do to get all the supplies for the horses had kept him from stressing over her disappearance. The physical labor of getting the stalls ready and hauling in hay and straw helped him catch a few hours of sleep at night.

"If they'd been abandoned, were they okay when you brought them here?" she asked.

"Yeah, Brody's large-animal vet came and checked them out."

She swallowed and her eyes shimmered with what looked like unshed tears. *Damn*. He needed to steer this conversation away from himself or he'd be taking her in his arms again. "Have you ever thought about taking over the administrative running of the program?"

"Me? Why would you think I could do something like that?"

He shrugged. "You know a lot about it and you work miracles."

"Miracles?" Her head snapped back "What makes you think I work miracles?"

"You not only got me into town during December but also got me to eat at the café like a regular person." And she had him questioning why he'd given up all his hopes and dreams, setting them aside as if they had meant nothing.

"And the world didn't come to an end! Now, that's a miracle."

He reached over and flicked the end of her nose. "You're going to be ruining my reputation. I won't be able to growl at people and have them run in fright."

She laughed. "It's like a *Scooby-Doo* episode. I lifted the sheet and underneath all that frightening bluster was simply a grumpy man trying to scare people away."

"At least you didn't say grumpy *old* man."

"No, sir, I wouldn't do that."

"Careful or I'll…" He stared at her lips, plump from his kisses.

"You'll what?" she asked in a breathless challenge, her chin at a pert angle.

Did she want him to kiss her again as much as he wanted to? He started to lower his head, but one of the five horses kicked against the stall.

"We have an audience," he muttered, regaining his senses. Had he lost his mind? What was he doing repeating mistakes? And that first kiss had been a mistake. Hadn't it? Of course it had because it left him wanting more. More kisses, more everything.

"We do," she agreed and sighed. She checked her

watch. "I need to go, but I promise I'll be back bright and early tomorrow to care for the horses."

She put her hands on her hips. "I thought you said you wouldn't end up like Brody, taking in unwanted animals."

He scowled. "Did I?"

Her expression softened and she leaned closer. "You know you did."

Before he could give in to temptation again, he held out his hand. "Give me your cell phone."

"My phone? Why?" she asked but reached into her jacket pocket and pulled it out.

He put his hands on his hips to keep from snatching the phone from her hand. "So I can program my number in. In case you…uh, in case you need to contact me."

At first she looked confused, then her eyes widened and she nodded. "Oh, right. Of course you'll need my number because of the horses."

That would be a plausible, safe excuse, but it would be a lie. And when push came to shove, he couldn't lie to her. He shook his head. "I want it so you can let me know next time you go out of town."

"Did…did you miss me?" She handed him her phone.

"I didn't say that." He didn't look up from the screen as he programmed his number into her contacts. He hated to admit this, but if she hadn't shown up today, he'd planned to go into town and talk to Tavie—of all people—to ask where Natalie and Sam lived. He'd needed to reassure himself that they were both okay. He never would have lived it down with Tavie, but that was how desperate he'd become by day three.

She grinned. "You didn't have to."

He grunted and handed her back the phone, but when she reached for it he captured her hand and tugged her closer. Raising his head, he looked at the horse stalls. "Any objections?"

Augie snorted and whinnied, shaking his head as if he'd understood the question.

"Tough," Des muttered to the opinionated horse and cupped his hands around Natalie's face.

He gently brushed his thumbs across her cheeks as his lips touched hers again. She tasted like peppermint and new beginnings. It was then that he knew he was lost. And he didn't care. If this was lost, he never wanted to be found.

Natalie was lost in the kiss. His lips were firm and gentle and she craved what he was doing to her. She groaned and he pressed closer, letting her feel what she did to him. She reveled in that knowledge.

One of the horses whinnied and stamped its foot, breaking the spell. She sighed and pulled away. It was for the best, she told herself, but it hurt all the same. She took a step back.

"I don't want to, but I need to go," she said and licked her lips. He'd kissed all the lip gloss off them.

"Why the rush?"

She tried to decipher his expression. Did she detect hurt? Did she have that much power? "I—I can't stay. I need to get ready for tonight."

"Hot date?" he asked, his voice tight, his eyes dark.

She shook her head, meeting his gaze straight on. "I promised Sam we'd go to the town tree-lighting to-night. He was worried we'd missed it when we were in

Boston. I assured him we didn't, so I have to keep my promise to take him."

He cleared his throat. "Am I still invited?"

She reached up and cupped his cheek, his scruff scratching her palm. All her nerve endings tingled at the touch. "Of course. Sam will be thrilled. Do you want to pick a time and spot to meet up?"

He shook his head. "Give me your address and I'll pick you up."

She told him where she lived and he walked her back to her car.

He opened her door but touched her arm, preventing her from getting in. "I'm glad you're back."

"Me, too."

"Who told you the horses were here?"

"No one."

"Then why did you come out here?"

Heat crept up her face and settled in her cheeks. "When I found out the horses were gone…coming here was my first reaction. I felt an overpowering need to talk to you."

She searched his face for a clue as to how he felt about her admission.

He tucked strands of hair behind her ear. "I'm glad."

Later that day Des pulled into Natalie's working-class neighborhood of older but well-loved homes. The pleasant, well-lit street ended in a cul-de-sac, the dead end a plus for families with young children like Natalie. His GPS indicated Natalie's was coming up on the left: one of two duplexes on the street, the home had brick on the bottom and blue clapboards on the upper

half. It was set back from the road and had a decent-
sized front yard. A cement sidewalk led to three steps
and a small covered entry with an overhead light shining down on the entrance. The black door and window
shutters gleamed as if freshly painted.

He pulled into the blacktop driveway and shut off
the engine. He stared at Natalie's house, thinking about
the woman inside, and the last time he'd been on a date.
Date? But this wasn't a date. Would she see it that way?
They were taking Sam to the town tree-lighting, that
was all. More of a community thing they were doing
together. They were both attending anyway, so together
made sense, really. *You were going, anyway?* If not for
Natalie and Sam, he wouldn't have been caught dead
anywhere near the town square this evening. And yet,
he'd been looking forward to this outing after talking
with Natalie in the barn. Talking? *More like kissing.*

He got out of his truck and went to the front door. An
evergreen wreath with a giant red velvet bow hung on
the inner black painted door. He could picture her placing the wreath with that appealing smile, asking Sam
if he liked it. And Sam giving his thumbs-up, smile in
place and his blue eyes bright. Before he could ring the
bell, the inner door opened, disturbing the wreath. His
breath caught in his throat at the sunny smile that lit up
her face and reached her eyes.

"Hi, c'mon in." She opened the glass storm door.

He stepped inside, caught the outer door so it didn't
bang, then closed the inner one. The front entrance
opened into a small but cheerful living room. Shoes
were lined up by the door, a stack of Harry Potter books

and magazines piled on the coffee table and miniature cars and LEGOs scattered on the floor.

"Sorry we're not ready. The kitten ran away with one of Sam's mittens and we've been searching for it."

"The kitten or the mitten?"

"Both. I bet you weren't expecting to walk into a nursery rhyme, huh?" A giggle bubbled out. "You look confused. I was referring to the Mother Goose rhyme about three little kittens who lost their mittens. I used to read it to Sam."

He swallowed, thinking how cheerful Natalie's home was compared to his. His might be larger and not as cluttered, but Natalie's place was warm and inviting. His? Not so much. Could Natalie and Sam bring their warmth and cheerful chaos to his place? He scowled. Ever since she'd barged into his barn that day, Natalie had been messing with his head. She'd made him want things, made him think things were possible.

Blushing, she wrung her hands together. "It's okay to say 'Natalie, shut up' if my chatter starts to get on your nerves."

Damn. She must've interpreted his silence negatively. He reached out to stop her hand-wringing by taking one of hers in his. He stroked her palm with his thumb. "That's not what I was thinking. I apologize if I gave you the wrong impression."

He pulled her closer so their bodies were practically touching. Gazing into her eyes, he saw an emotion lurking in their blue depths. It looked like hurt and he hated that he might have put it there. "It's not what I was thinking at all."

"You had one of those mightily menacing scowls of

yours going on." She swallowed and shifted, bringing herself even closer to him. "So tell me what you were thinking."

Mightily menacing? He shook his head, disturbed that she saw him like that. "I was thinking that—"

Sam came running down the hall followed by a black-and-silver tabby jumping up, trying to grab a mitten in his hand. Sam giggled as he tried to keep the mitten away from the lunging cat.

Des threw Natalie a surprised look.

She met his gaze. "I don't hear that sound often enough. But I've heard it more since we've had the kitten and he's been in hippotherapy. As happy as he was to get spoiled by his grandmother, he missed that crazy cat while we were in Boston."

She laid her hand on Sam's shoulder. "Put your jacket on, please. You were supposed to be ready when Mr. Des got here."

Sam looked up at him, those big eyes so like Natalie's, and thrust out his lower lip. Des felt as if his insides were melting.

Des rubbed a hand over his mouth to hide his smile. "Better do as your mom says," he told him but winked and was rewarded with a giant grin.

Des reached down to pet the cat, who was busy sniffing his pants. "Hey, there, what's…?" He glanced at Natalie.

"His name's Shadow." She hunkered down and got the zipper on Sam's jacket started. "Because he was Sam's shadow from the moment we got him."

She scooped up the cat and cradled it close to her chest. The kitten huddled closer and nuzzled Natalie's neck.

"Wow, I never knew they could purr that loud," Des said. Not that he could blame the kitten. He'd be purring, too, if she was letting him snuggle her neck, her subtle lavender scent filling his nostrils.

"Yeah, he's a regular motorboat. Let me put him in the kitchen and give him some treats and a toy. It'll distract him while we leave. He's an indoor cat." She disappeared into the kitchen, cuddling the animal. "Sam, put your mittens on," she called from the other room.

She came back without the cat and picked up her giant purse and slung the straps over her shoulder. Outside, she got Sam's booster seat out of her Camry and secured it in the backseat of the truck. Sam was bouncing on the balls of his feet as he waited. He tugged on Des's sleeve.

That laugh made his chest expand and Des couldn't stop grinning. He was as proud of Sam as he would be of his own son.

Sam handed the tablet back to Natalie, who slipped it into her purse. Sam climbed into the truck, and she double-checked that the booster seat was secure. Des hurried to the front passenger side and opened her door.

"So you're an officer and a gentleman," she said.

He grunted. "The door sometimes sticks and you have to maneuver the handle just right."

She shook her head. "Why do you fight it so much?"

"What do you mean?"

"You don't want me to see you as an admirable man."

"I'm simply saving you future disappointment." Was he that transparent? He had been trying to keep some space between them.

"I can't imagine ever being disappointed in you."

"Give it time," he said and shut her door.

After leaving Natalie's place, he drove to Main Street and found a parking spot in the church's lot. They got out of the truck, crossed the parking lot and headed toward the festivities on the town square.

"Sam, it's crowded here tonight. You need to hold my hand."

After watching other boys darting around, Sam shook his head. He crossed his arms over his chest, tucking his hands into his armpits.

"Sam," Natalie said in a warning tone laced with frustration.

Des understood the boy's reluctance, but he wanted to tell Sam how lucky he was to have a mother who was so concerned about him. Except he couldn't do that without going into stuff he wasn't about to get into with anyone, even Natalie. Instead, he held out his own hand. "Would you hold mine?"

Sam's eyes widened and he uncrossed his arms, holding out his hand.

"Do you mind?" Natalie asked, sounding surprised.

Des couldn't blame her; he'd surprised himself with the offer.

"Of course not," Des said and took Sam's hand. His heart squeezed when the boy grinned shyly up at him. *Oh, man, don't look up to me, kiddo. If your mom knew how messed up I am, she'd be running away and taking you with her.*

They crossed the street and entered the crowd on the green.

"Are you guys warm enough?" Des asked as they made their way to the front of the crowd so Sam would have a better view. "I know this is your first real taste of winter."

"I will have you know, Lieutenant Gallagher, that we had winters in Nashville."

He barked a laugh. "Yeah, right."

She playfully poked him. "You laugh, but I guarantee we're here to stay."

"A promise and not a threat, right?"

She rolled her eyes at him, but she had that giant grin he enjoyed and her eyes sparkled. He not only enjoyed that smile but also rejoiced at putting it there.

Despite standing near the front, Sam was jumping up, trying to get a better view of the tree, so Natalie adjusted her purse straps on her shoulder and started to bend down to pick him up.

"Let me," Des said and put a hand on her arm to stop her. He then swung up Sam and put him on his shoulders, hanging on to his feet. "That better, bud?"

"He's nodding." Natalie patted her son's leg.

A choral group sang several Christmas carols with the high school band accompanying as a prelude to the tree-lighting.

The mayor stepped up to the podium. "We're going to light this tree in a minute but first I want to urge everyone to stay and enjoy refreshments provided by the town's restaurants. Our businesses are donating tonight's proceeds to the high school music program."

He then went over to the ceremonial switch and pulled it with an exaggerated flourish. The huge evergreen came alive with thousands of twinkling lights and the crowd cheered.

Sam clapped and bounced with excitement, causing Des to tighten his grip on the boy.

Des set Sam back on the ground and took his hand. "How about something hot to warm up? That sound good to you, Sam?"

Attracted by the smells of cinnamon and warm dough, they strolled over to a booth that served hot cider, hot chocolate and doughnuts.

As they waited in the long line, an older man tapped Natalie on the shoulder. "Natalie, hi. Glad I ran into you. Saves me a phone call."

She turned and greeted him. "Hey, Mitch. Good to see you, too. Do you know Des Gallagher? Des, this is Mitch Makowski."

Mitch stuck out his hand. "You're the fella who rescued Natalie's horses."

Des shook Mitch's hand. "Well, I—"

"They're hardly *my* horses, Mitch." Natalie shook her head.

"Whatever." Mitch waved his hand. "My neighbor's grandson has benefited from that program, so I know they do good work. You still taking donations for that auction of yours?"

"Yes, we're always on the lookout for more items now that the horses are safe. Pastor Cook has been kind enough to let us use the church storage shed until the auction. Do you have something?"

"My wife's sister sold painted wood crafts at local flea markets for years, but she's packing it in. Moving to Florida to enjoy retirement. Anyway, she's got a bunch of Christmas things she's willing to donate. Even the artificial trees she used to display them."

"That sounds great. We might even be able to auction the trees as is."

"That's what she thought. Only catch is, you'll have to pick them up. I don't suppose you have a pickup." Mitch glanced at Des before turning back to Natalie.

"Hmm, maybe I could ask Br—"

"We'll use mine," Des said. The words were out of his mouth before his brain could stop them.

"We could?" Natalie turned to him.

Mitch pulled out a business card and handed it to Natalie. "Give her a call if you want to set something up."

"Thanks, Mitch. I appreciate this." Natalie shook his hand.

"Glad to help out with a good cause." The older man grinned and wiggled his bushy, snow-white eyebrows. "And I knew your grandmother back in the day. Sorry to lose her so soon."

"Thank you." Natalie gave Mitch one of her special smiles.

They moved forward a few paces in line as Des wondered what had gotten into him. Since he'd moved to Loon Lake, he'd done his best to avoid interactions with the residents. And yet, here he was, offering to drive around and do just that.

She put the business card in her purse. "You're sure you don't mind helping?"

"I offered, didn't I?" Exactly why did he? He glanced at Natalie. Ha, that was easy. It was a chance to spend more time with her and Sam, to be a part of her world, bask in the glow of her smile.

"Yes, you did, but that didn't answer my question."

Yeah, because he didn't want to admit that he had his own selfish reasons for offering to help. Did he want to admit that to her right now? "Are you always this gracious when someone offers to help?"

She glanced sharply at him as they stepped forward. "Are you saying I'm not acting gracious?"

"You seem reluctant. Is this how you normally act?" He hadn't meant to anger her, just deflect.

"No." She sighed and grinned. "Normally, I would smile and say thank you."

"So I'm an exception?" Why was he pressing her? Did he really want to know how she felt?

She tilted her head and placed her open palm across his chest. "You are. Does that bother you?"

His heart pounded under her palm as if trying to get to her. "No, but I am curious as to why."

Her smile held a hint of sadness. "Don't you think you're an exceptional person?"

"Exceptional? Me?" He rolled his eyes and shook his head, but in that moment he longed to be that man she saw. Could he? "That's stretching things a bit."

They reached the front of the line and Des ordered three hot chocolates and a bag of mini-doughnuts. After getting their order, he carried the cardboard tray over to a spot that had been set up with long tables and chairs.

Natalie made sure Sam was settled with his drink and doughnut before sitting. "So you're okay with helping collect auction items? Boarding the horses is above and beyond."

He took the cover off his drink. "I offered so I'll do it."

She exhaled. "The truth is, I didn't want you to feel

as if you'd been put on the spot in front of Mitch. You know, saying you'd help to be nice."

"Wow." He snapped his head back in mock surprise, but couldn't hide his grin. "That's the first time I've been accused of being nice."

She gave him a thoughtful assessment. "Well, I think it's better if people are honest about their feelings. You don't have to be cruel but honesty is important."

He shook his head, the humor evaporating. "Honesty in relationships in overrated."

Her jaw dropped. "How can you even say something like that?"

It's easy when your own mother tells you things you never wanted to know. In the days following Patrick's suicide, their mother had made it clear that when her favorite son had died she'd lost the only link to the man she'd worshipped—the man who'd been Patrick's father but not his. Weeks later she'd offered a stiff apology, saying she'd voiced sentiments in the depths of grief that she shouldn't have. Although he'd accepted it, he couldn't help notice that the apology was for voicing her feelings, not for having them or that they weren't true. "Because once something is out there, you can't take it back."

"But if you keep your feelings hidden, that can cause problems, too."

"Those problems are nothing compared to the ones that honesty can cause." And he should know. He grew up, knowing no matter what he did, he couldn't hold the same place in his mother's heart as Patrick. And Ashley came along and let him know he was interchangeable with whatever man could give her the future she'd envisioned.

"I guess we'll have to agree to disagree." Natalie touched his arm. "Let's not let a difference of opinion spoil this fun night."

He put his hand over hers on his arm. "So you're having a good time?"

She nodded. "Yes. Aren't you?"

More fun than he'd had in a long, long time. "I'm getting a kick out of watching you two enjoy it."

"Then I'm glad you came with us."

Sam's eyes started to droop as soon as he'd finished his doughnut and hot chocolate. Des squeezed Natalie's hand and when she met his gaze, he hitched his chin toward Sam.

"Ready to go?" she asked as she began gathering up their trash. "I think we're all tired."

Sam's eyes popped open and he shook his head.

"You need to get your rest so we can go to the lieutenant's tomorrow and take care of the horses," she told him.

Sam straightened up and looked to Des for confirmation.

"That's right." Des snapped his fingers and pointed to Sam. "I'll be needing all the help I can get taking care of those horses. Are you up to it, Sam?"

His eyes wide with excitement, Sam nodded.

"Then we all need a good night's sleep and you can come over bright and early with your mom," Des told him and stood up with the trash. He had plenty of competent potential help lined up, but Sam was so excited he didn't have the heart to tell him his wasn't necessary. "But be ready to work hard."

Sam laughed and jumped out of his seat and raced around the table toward Des. When he reached Des, Sam threw his arms around him. The cardboard tray with the trash wobbled and Natalie grabbed it. Des patted Sam's back, trying to swallow the sudden clog in his throat. He might not deserve the boy's devotion, but he decided he'd do his best to live up to it.

Chapter Five

Sam had fallen fast asleep in the backseat by the time they'd gotten back to Natalie's place.

"I'll carry him in," Des told her when he pulled into her driveway.

He opened the rear door and leaned in. He unbuckled the restraints and lifted a sleeping Sam out of the booster seat. The child wasn't heavy but his weight caused a strange new sensation in Des's chest—around the area of his heart. He'd never been around young children and wouldn't be if he remained single. He didn't have nieces or nephews to interact with. A lot of the men his age in Loon Lake had started or were adding to families, but Des only knew them in passing. A nod hello here and there but that was all. Not enough to interact.

When they'd been together, he and Ashley hadn't gotten around to discussing children. Huh, maybe that right there was a warning sign that their relationship was doomed. How could they have contemplated marriage without discussing something so important? He glanced down at Sam and clutched him a little tighter. At least he and Ashley hadn't brought an innocent child into their lives because their relationship hadn't weathered its first storm. He'd met Ashley while out in a group with fellow officers. They were all celebrating getting their various assignments. At the time, he'd considered their meeting a lucky coincidence. Now, the cynic in him wondered how much calculation had gone into that night, along with her easy acceptance of all the difficulties his training posed for a relationship.

Had he let his need for acceptance blind him to their problems?

He shifted Sam's weight in his arms and followed Natalie to the door. She unlocked it and pushed it open and stepped aside so he could go first.

"Could you bring him straight to his room?" Natalie whispered, then put her hand on his arm. "Wait a sec."

She leaned down and scooped up the black-and-silver cat. "He likes to trip people when they're carrying something and can't look down."

"I suppose it wouldn't be any fun otherwise," he whispered and was rewarded with one of her crooked-tooth smiles.

She followed him into Sam's bedroom and set the cat on the bed. The tabby walked around the bed and began kneading his claws on a royal blue fleece with orange moons and white spaceships.

"Let me get some of Sam's clothes off before you put him down."

Des nodded and she pulled off Sam's boots, hat and mittens. Des shifted and held the boy so she could unzip his jacket.

She pulled back the covers. "You can lay him down and I'll slip off the coat."

Des laid Sam on the bed. Natalie pulled off his jacket and put a ragged stuffed rabbit next to him before pulling up the blankets. He stirred and hugged the rabbit to his chest. The cat curled up next to the stuffed rabbit.

She smoothed the hair back from Sam's forehead in a tender gesture. "Bunny Rabbit kept him company when he was hospitalized."

Des watched her with her son. What would it be like to have her touch him as a lover? To have those hands explore him as they learned one another's bodies. Then afterward, for her to get that soft look in those big blue eyes as they—

Damn. What was wrong with him? He shook his head. Had he lost his mind? A warm, loving woman like Natalie deserved the same from a man and he'd already told her he didn't believe in everlasting love. Because he didn't. And he wasn't going to let Natalie change his mind. Was he?

Pushing away the things he felt watching her, he said, "I guess I should be heading out."

She gave him a puzzled look at his gruff tone. "Do you have to go already?"

Did he? "Well, I..."

She touched his arm. "Please. Have a seat in the living room."

He nodded and went into the other room, but instead of sitting he prowled restlessly around the cluttered room. He stopped in front of a framed photo of Natalie, a baby he assumed was Sam and a smiling man who must've been Natalie's husband, Sam's father. He had no business being jealous of a dead man. That was low and he should be ashamed of himself.

He took a last look at the photo, yearning for something he'd never had and never would. Or could he? For the first time since punching out of the cockpit of his F/A-18 he was starting to see a future that involved something more than what he had. A future that held more than what he'd had with Ashley. A future with a woman like Natalie, kids and—

"He's out like a light." Natalie came into the living room.

He'd turned at the sound of her voice, and once again he felt that tug around his heart. What was wrong with him? He was a man of logic, not emotions. In order to make it through those dark days following Patrick's suicide, he'd had to lock down his emotions. Soon it became habit, especially when his mother had started drinking and made it clear she'd lost the wrong son. How many times had he heard that Patrick's dad had been the love of her life? As if it had been his fault who his biological father was.

At first he'd chosen the navy because Patrick's father had been a career naval officer. But he found concentrating on a goal helped to block out his untenable situation with his mother. Then the rigid structure of the military became a haven.

"Des?"

He blinked and shoved the past aside, where it belonged. "Sorry, what did you say?"

"I asked if I could interest you in something?"

Yes, but not with anything I'm willing to voice out loud. What if he'd misinterpreted this whole situation? "Like what?"

"I have coffee, tea, hot cocoa or…" She grinned. "I have a bottle of Baileys if you want an adult version of hot chocolate."

"I'm not sure that's a good idea."

"Oh." Her disappointment was obvious in the confused look she gave him.

He put his finger to her lips. "I was thinking about the fact that I have to drive home."

She put her hands on his chest and gave him a shy smile. "Well, there's nothing that says you have to leave as soon as you drink it. I'm sure we could think of something to keep us occupied while you let the alcohol work its way out of your system."

He raised his eyebrows and stared into the depths of her eyes. "Are you sure? Because I'm not the kind of guy who—"

She silenced him by pressing her fingers to his lips. "Tonight let's pretend you're the kind of guy who sits and watches a movie with a woman on her sofa."

Okay. Not what he'd been imagining, but now he wanted nothing more than to watch a movie with her.

He gave her a quick kiss. "That sounds like fun. Did you have a movie in mind?"

She blushed and pointed to a small collection of movies sitting on a round table at the end of the couch. "I pulled out my Christmas movies the other day, but feel free to pick whatever kind you want. I have nonholiday ones on the shelf over there." She nodded at the built-in bookcases next to the television.

"Let me get the drinks started," she said.

"Do you want some help?"

"No, I'm good. Pick out a movie." She disappeared into the kitchen.

Watching a cheesy Christmas movie was the last thing he wanted, but if it meant sitting next to Natalie, he'd put up with the saccharine sentimentality.

He looked through her collection of holiday titles, pulled one out and grinned. He'd put the DVD into the player when she came and stood in the doorway between the kitchen and living room. The light from the kitchen glinted on her hair and he had the urge to run his hands through it and capture a bunch of strands in his fist while he—

"Did you find one?"

"Hmm?" He reined in his wayward thoughts and tried to concentrate on her question, but all he wanted was to kiss her senseless.

"A movie? Did you pick one out?" She squinted at him.

That was right. As much as he longed to kiss her, he also wanted to sit next to her while watching a movie. "Yup. I figured it must be one you like since it was in your stack of holiday films."

"Let me guess." She put her hands on her hips. "You didn't pick *The Holiday* or *While You Were Sleeping*."

"Uh, would you rather one of those?" He had no desire to watch either one of those, but he'd do it if it meant sitting next to her for the next ninety or so minutes.

"No. *Die Hard* is fine," she said and laughed.

"Hey, how do you know that's what I picked?"

She lowered her chin as she studied him. "Did you?"

He couldn't hide his grin. "Yeah."

"Let me get the drinks," she said before leaving the room.

He frowned. Was she regretting inviting him to stay? Before he could say anything, she reappeared, carrying mugs topped with whipped cream, a cinnamon stick stuck in each one. He took the one she offered.

They settled on the sofa and he rested his arm along the back, his fingers brushing her soft hair. He couldn't remember the last time he'd enjoyed an evening as much as this one. She took a sip of her drink as the movie began, then set the mug back on the small coffee table in front of them and snuggled against him. Her tongue darted out and licked off the whipped cream mustache and he groaned.

She looked up. "Something wrong?"

He brushed his finger along the corner of her mouth. "You missed a spot."

"You did, too." She reached up and skimmed around his lips with a featherlight touch.

"I better make sure," he murmured and leaned down.

As his lips brushed across hers, a small bundle of fur landed in his lap. What the...? The cat began to stroke its head across his chest and purr.

He straightened but kept his arm around Natalie's shoulder, anchoring her to his side. The cat curled up on his lap and settled in. "What did you say his name was?"

"Shadow. Why?"

He grunted. "Are you sure it's not Chaperone?"

She laughed and snuggled closer as the movie started. He sighed and scowled at Shadow, who looked up and slowly blinked at him. If he didn't know better, he'd swear the cat was smirking at him.

Halfway through the movie, Des noticed Natalie's breathing had evened out. He glanced down at her asleep against his side and grinned. He let the rest of the movie play but his attention was on the woman sleeping next to him. He ran his fingertip along her cheek and tucked strands of hair behind her ear. She smiled in her sleep and burrowed closer with a sigh.

As the movie was ending, she awoke with a start and startled the cat, who dug his claws into Des's thigh before jumping down to stalk off.

"This is embarrassing." She sat up and yawned. "Sorry. I guess I wasn't much company."

Des chuckled and touched the mark on her cheek from the button on his shirt pocket. "I thought I might have to carry you to bed and tuck you in like Sam."

She blushed. "I'm sorry."

"I didn't mind." And he found that he didn't. He enjoyed being with Natalie.

The following morning, Natalie drove to Des's place, dressed for mucking out the stables or whatever else she needed to do. She'd been serious about helping with the horses and so had Sam. He'd been raring to go from the moment he got up. Jiggling in his seat as he ate his oatmeal. She wasn't sure who he was more excited to see, Des or Augie. As much as she wanted to see the horses, Des was the bigger draw for her. No question about it.

Warmth rose in her face as she recalled dozing off

while cuddled up to Des last night. Despite that embarrassment, she'd enjoyed spending the evening on the sofa with Des as much as any date in a fancy restaurant.

Des must've heard them pull up because he was waiting in the doorway to the barn when they drove up and parked.

He came over as she turned off the engine and opened her door. "Good morning."

"Good morning. Your helpers have arrived," she said and got out of the car. "I hope you haven't started having all the fun of mucking stables without us."

He laughed and opened Sam's door. "Not a chance."

"Good because we're ready to work hard. As a matter of fact, if you want to work on your art, we can handle this."

He chuckled. "I'm sure both of you are eager and willing to help, but be warned, caring for horses is no easy task."

She swallowed. Didn't he want them there? He'd seemed keen on the idea last night. "I don't think it's fair to you to have to do everything."

"Don't fret. When I agreed to help, Brody offered to share his stable hands if necessary and one of them, Kevin, has already been here this morning to get us started. And I'm sure with Sam's help we'll be done in no time if you two have plans for later."

"As a matter of fact, we're going to look for a Christmas tree. A couple people on the street already have theirs up. Of course they probably have fake trees, but Tavie said the garden center will have the freshest trees, so we'll check there first to see if they have any yet."

"Even those will have been cut down a while ago," Des said as they made their way into the barn.

She laughed. "Unless we go chop one down ourselves, I guess we'll run into that."

He handed her a pair of work gloves. "To help prevent blisters if you're not used to raking."

"Thanks." She took them.

Sam held up his hands and Des laughed. "I didn't forget you, buddy."

He pulled out a pair of child-sized gloves from his pocket. "Specially for you."

Natalie swallowed, remembering the first time they'd come to the barn. He'd been brusque with them, but she'd been right to sense something more underneath that crusty exterior. She'd been a little afraid that first day. And now? The thing that scared her was how much she was beginning to care for him.

"Were you interested in chopping down a Christmas tree?" Des asked as they started cleaning out the stalls. With advice from the therapy center employees as to which horses got along, he'd sent the them into the various fenced paddocks before Sam and Natalie arrived.

"As wonderful as that sounds, I fear we may have to settle for a garden center tree." She had even debated on getting an artificial tree, but for their first Christmas in Loon Lake she wanted to go all out. Sam was getting older and the time was coming when he'd consider himself too old for many of the traditions they enjoyed now.

"I have quite a bit of wooded property here. I'm sure we can find a suitable tree and it's best to do it today before the snow makes it more difficult to go tramping in the woods."

"For real? You'd do that for us?" Every time she thought she had Des figured out, he surprised her. "Sam and I thank you."

Sam gave an enthusiastic thumbs-up.

After they'd finished cleaning the stall that hadn't been touched yet, they took a break in the workshop then followed Des to his truck.

"We'll drive out to the edge of the trees. There's a dirt road that leads down there," he explained.

"Do you go into the woods much?"

"Why? You thinking you need to leave a trail of breadcrumbs?" He put his hands on his hips.

"Should I? You haven't built a gingerbread house in there, have you?"

He looked confused and she scolded herself for yet another children's story reference. *For crying out loud, he's a grown man with no kids, Natalie.*

Heat rose in her face. "*Hansel and Gretel* ring any bells?"

"Ah. The old witch with the oven."

"Yes. See, you remember."

He laughed and opened a rear door for Sam. "More like a good guess."

"I'm planning to make a gingerbread house for Sam and me to decorate." She climbed into the passenger seat.

"That I've got to see," Des said before he shut her door.

"We'll let you know when it's done, won't we, Sam?" She turned to look into the back.

"I'll hold you to it," he said as he slipped behind the wheel and started the engine.

The truck spewed up gravel behind it as he drove along the dirt road toward the tree line.

"So you've never cut down your own tree before?" he asked.

"No. In the past Sam and I would walk around the garden center attached to the big home improvement store, checking out trees that had been cut at least a month before."

Des brought the truck to a stop near the tree line. They piled out of the truck and Des retrieved an ax. She and Sam followed him into the woods.

"Pick out your tree, bud." He adjusted Sam's knit cap. "This one may not be perfect like the cultivated ones, but it will definitely be fresh."

"You're right." She took a deep breath and released a contented sigh. "It even smells like Christmas out here."

She turned her face up and frowned. A few wispy clouds spread across the blue sky, not the kind that foretold of snow, the one thing this holiday was missing.

"You'll get your fill of snow soon enough." Des elbowed her and chuckled.

The hair on the back of her neck stood up at the sexy sound. "I was promised snow."

"You don't want snow today. We need to get your tree first." He hitched his chin toward Sam. "He's taking this task quite seriously."

She nodded, blinking back sudden tears. Des had made this possible and she would be forever grateful. As much as he tried to make everyone believe he was a Scrooge, his generosity told a different story. And she was falling for him, even the grumpy parts. She prayed she wasn't making a mistake, but then her heart seemed to have a mind of its own when it came to Des.

"He's safe out here," he said, interrupting her thoughts.

She lifted her face up to look at him. Had he seen her tearing up? "What do you mean?"

"You don't have a death grip on his hand today." He motioned his head toward Sam, who was examining each tree, no matter how big or small. "But I see how nervous you are."

Let him think that was the cause of her tears. She wasn't ready to admit her innermost thoughts and feelings yet. "Am I that obvious?"

"I can't say I blame you." He reached out his hand. "You can hold my hand if it will make you feel better."

"Are you in danger of wandering off?" She laughed, enjoying his playful mood.

"You never know." He held up his hand.

"Then perhaps I'd better." She took his hand, her skin tingling when it made contact with his.

As they followed Sam on his quest for the perfect tree, she explained about the time she'd lost track of him in the department store. "So now I keep a death grip on his hand."

"I wasn't criticizing." He lifted her hand to his mouth and pressed his lips against her knuckles. "I can't imagine how difficult it must be."

"Thanks." She had trouble concentrating with his lips on her skin. "I'm grateful he survived the accident and how far he's come, but I still worry."

Des put his arm around her. "Are you warm enough? I imagine you Southern gals have to get used to our winters."

She shivered but not from the cold; it was his deep voice and warm breath so close to her ear. "I'm fine. I'm learning to dress in layers. I started with thermal underwear. First time I've worn it. Probably not sexy but it keeps me warm."

"Maybe that calls for a second opinion." His mesmerizing gaze lingered on her lips.

Her heart thudded under his dark-eyed gaze. "To be sure I'm wearing it correctly?"

"Call me quality control." He grinned and squeezed her against his side.

"Oh, I can think of a lot of names to call you," she teased, enjoying the lighter side of him. So much different from the side he'd shown her that first day. But still, she'd seen past that facade, because he'd stayed on her mind all day and into the evening.

"Ouch." He brought their linked hands to his chest.

"Hey, who said they were bad names?" Having fun, she batted her eyes and adopted a drawl. "Why, Lieutenant, I think you're projecting."

"Have I told you how much I love listening to you?"

"You like the accent?"

"I do indeed." He bumped her shoulder and pointed toward Sam, who was stopped in front of an evergreen that had to be ten feet tall and nearly as wide. He glanced back at them with a hopeful expression.

She smiled. "It's beautiful but it's way too big for our living room, I'm afraid. Look for something smaller."

Sam nodded and ran ahead, stopping every so often to examine a tree.

"He's enjoying this. Thanks." She leaned against Des, enjoying being in his company. He made tramping through the woods special. "You're being a good sport, considering you don't even like Christmas."

He shook his head. "Walking around my property isn't a hardship. Uh-oh, looks like he found one."

"That one?" Her dismay came through in her tone.

Des glanced at her and turned back to Sam. "Are you sure that's the one you want, bud?"

Sam nodded his head and reached over and touched the tree again.

"We can get something a bit bigger," she told him. How was she going to handle this? She sighed.

Sam shook his head, touching the tree again.

"Serves me right for reading *The Littlest Christmas Tree* to him," she whispered to Des.

He chuckled, showing no sympathy. "It'll be fine once you get lights and decorations on it."

Says the man who dislikes Christmas. "It will still be a Charlie Brown tree."

"Look how happy he is," Des whispered back and winked. He glanced in Sam's direction and leaned down and gave her a kiss. "That's important, isn't it?"

"I suppose." She shrugged and struggled for an explanation. "I wanted this Christmas to be perfect."

"Why?"

"Because it's our first year in Loon Lake." That sounded lame even to her. She couldn't put her finger on why this was so important. Was it because this was their first year in Loon Lake? Or did her reasons run deeper than she was willing to admit?

He turned and stood in front of her. "His challenges aren't your fault," he said quietly.

"What?" How could he know what she'd been thinking? "What are you saying?"

"I think you're bending over backward to make up for the hand life has dealt your son."

"I'm his mother." She shook her head. "I'm supposed to take care of him."

"You are. Look at him." Des pointed to Sam, who was walking around the tree as if he couldn't believe his luck in finding it. "He may not be able to speak, but he communicates. And he knows he's loved by you. From what I've seen, he's well adjusted."

She sighed. Des made a lot of sense, but it was still hard for her not to want to hold Sam and be able to make everything better. She knew he would be facing numerous challenges in the years to come, and the thought made her heart ache. "I confess I'm worried about what will happen when he starts school. I won't be there to protect him. I need to get a job, so homeschooling is out and I'm not sure I should. Maybe being around other kids more is what he needs."

Des put his arm around her shoulder and pulled her close. "You're giving him a solid background…a loving home to help him navigate life's ups and downs. Don't beat yourself up."

He kissed her temple.

"Thanks. I…"

"You what?" Des asked.

I think I'm falling for you. "Nothing."

The earth was shifting beneath her feet. Was she falling in love with Des? No, it was too soon. Love should take longer than this, be more gradual. This could be a crush, that's all. She swallowed the words before they could escape. He wouldn't be amenable to hearing them yet. And she wasn't ready, either. It was too soon for any big declaration.

Guilt burned in the back of her throat at the thought of falling in love again. Ryan had been dead for three years. No one could accuse her of moving on without a backward glance, and yet, loving another man was a big step. Was she ready to risk her heart again?

He gave her a quizzical look but didn't press and she was grateful. She wasn't ready to tell him something like that yet. She would have to get used to that herself. When had her feelings deepened? She'd been attracted to him from the start. Her feelings had been a mixture of lust and like for a while. And yes, some exasperation with him at times.

"So you're good?"

"Huh?" She needed to pay attention or risk having Des suspect something.

He pointed. "With the tree. I'll chop it down."

"That's right. We have to chop it down." She grimaced. The tree was, after all, a living thing.

"It's a tree, Natalie."

"I realize that." This was silly because this was the whole reason they'd come out here. She sighed. "It's up to Sam."

"Do you want to help me chop down your tree, Sam?" Des asked.

Sam did a thumbs-up and grinned.

"I see I've been overruled."

Des chuckled. "Would you have felt that way about chopping down a Hallmark-worthy tree?"

She crossed her arms. "No comment."

"We'll be giving this less than perfect tree a chance to shine. Like Cinderella." He grinned. "Looks like it's my turn to involve you in a children's story."

"You are way too clever." She elbowed him and laughed. "Okay. Okay. You've sold me, but I still need to get a stand and pull out all the ornaments from the basement before I can get it set up."

"It'll be fine once you get it decorated. You'll see," he whispered to her.

He chopped down the tree and Sam helped him carry it to the pickup. Seeing the look on Sam's face, she knew Des was right. She might have picked out a fuller tree with a better shape, but she had a feeling this tree would be a wonderful memory for Sam. And that had been part of her reason for moving to Loon Lake, to create lifelong memories for them both.

Des and Sam seemed to have bonded over the tree. Her stomach knotted. Ryan would never get the chance to do something like that with his son. That was sad, but she couldn't let regrets prevent Sam from enjoying moments like this. She did worry about Sam's growing attachment to Des, because his tender heart was at the mercy of the adults around him.

"I'll bring it to your place as soon as you're ready," Des told her as he closed the tailgate with a *thunk*.

Back at the farm, Des parked his truck next to her car and glanced into the mirror. "Come into the house. Sam looks like he could use some refreshments. How does that sound to you, Sam?"

Sam gave him a thumbs-up.

Natalie's gaze went from her son to Des. "You're offering refreshments?"

"I may not be Martha Stewart, but I have been known to do a little entertaining."

"This I've got to see," she teased.

"Are you insulting me? Because you didn't preface it with 'bless your heart.'"

She laughed and undid her seat belt. "Bless your heart, but by your own admission you've been chasing people away for the past three years."

"But that doesn't mean I don't know how to be a gracious host. I simply choose not to."

"Okay, point taken."

Des led them to the back door and into a mudroom paneled with bright white wooden panels, a brick floor and built-in benches on either side.

"Sam, honey, sit and take your boots off," Natalie said as she slipped off her own footwear. "Your mudroom is gorgeous. Puts mine to shame, that's for sure."

Des shrugged as he toed off his own boots after loosening the laces. "It was this way when I bought the house."

Boots in hand, Sam touched her arm and pointed to one of the cubbyholes under the bench across from the one she was sitting on.

"Is it okay if he puts his boots under there?" she asked and motioned toward the bench.

"Sure." Des picked up his own boots. "Here, I'll put mine next to yours, bud."

She put her hands on her hips as she faced Sam. "How come you're not this neat at home?"

Sam shrugged and giggled.

Natalie set her boots in the available space next to theirs and paused at the sight. Closing her eyes, she recalled childhood memories of placing her shoes next to her dad's giant army boots and her mom's ballet flats. But the three of them weren't a family and she needed to put the brakes on those thoughts. Sam's heart wasn't the only one in danger. She may have survived her grief when she lost Ryan, but her belief in fairy tales had been steadfast when she'd married him. Now, she understood love didn't protect people from life's tragedies.

Blinking and pushing aside the maudlin thoughts, she straightened and followed Sam and Des through the door into the kitchen.

Her gaze roamed around the beautiful but sparse kitchen. Raising an eyebrow, she asked, "Previous owner?"

Des chuckled. "Good guess."

Sam tugged on her sleeve and gave her a look.

"Bathroom?" she asked. When he nodded, she turned to Des. "Where's the bathroom?"

Des set the loaf of bread in his hands on the counter and pointed. "Through the dining room and into the front hall. First door on the left."

"Thanks. Let me show him."

She led Sam through an empty dining room and into a hall that led to the front of the house. After Sam closed the bathroom door, she glanced down the hall and drew in a sharp breath as her gaze landed on the stained glass inset in the front door. The colorful glass depicted a loon taking flight from a lake. Unable to resist, she went to the door and reached out to run her fingertips over the bird. She'd never seen such intricate stained glass work. Looking at it, she'd swear she could feel the disturbed air from its fluttering wings.

A man who created such inspiring beauty had to be capable of deep emotions, but being able wasn't the same as being willing. She herself was leery of opening herself once again to the vagaries of love. Des might be capable, but was he willing to open his heart? From what he'd told her, he might not be.

Des stepped into the doorway to the dining room and glanced down the hall. Standing at the front door, Natalie was tracing the stained glass insert he'd installed as soon as it was finished. Her fingers lingered on the depiction of the loon rising from the lake. It may have taken him numerous tries to get it perfect, but seeing her reaction made it all worthwhile. After all, she'd been his muse. She'd made him want to make what had started as a simple piece more complex, like her. And as close to perfection as he could get.

Des went through the dining room and into the hall to stand behind her. With his limp he wasn't exactly Mr. Stealth, but she hadn't turned around at his approach. Was she that engrossed in the piece?

"Like it?" Des asked from behind her.

She startled and turned to face him. "It's stunning. I'm going to assume you made it."

"Yeah." He shrugged, but pride made him puff his chest out. "Finished it recently and decided to keep it."

"Do you keep a lot of what you make?" She touched his arm as she spoke.

Her hand on his arm made the hair on the back of his neck stand up. In a good way. A very good way. "No. Very few, actually."

"But you kept this one. Why? I mean, it's beautiful,

but so are the ones Tavie sells in the General Store. That's where I first noticed them." She dropped her hand.

"I have my reasons." He wasn't about to admit that he'd feared he'd lost his muse until the day she showed up with her crooked-tooth smile and tin of candy. She'd inspired this piece and he couldn't part with it. No matter what happened between them, the piece would always hold special meaning for him.

"Are you always this mysterious?"

He lifted his chin as he contemplated her. "Wow, I've graduated from conundrum to mysterious? Is this a good thing? A step in the right direction?"

She crossed her arms. "What do you mean?"

This time he reached out to touch her. "Are women more apt to be attracted to mysterious as opposed to flat-out grumpy?"

She gave him a side eye. "Depends."

"On what?" He scowled, but was enjoying the verbal sparring. He couldn't remember the last time he'd liked being with someone as much as he did with her.

"On how well they entertain their company?"

The fact that she posed it as a question had him laughing. He couldn't help himself. She was charming and she had succeeded in charming him. No doubt about it. He was smitten.

She pointed at him. "You should do that more often."

"Entertain?" He didn't think that was what she meant, but he needed to know what she meant, hear her say it.

She shook her head. "Laugh. It makes you more… more…"

"More what?" He held his breath, waiting for her answer. Her opinion mattered to him. His gut clenched. What was he getting himself into? Did he want to leave himself open to the possibility of getting hurt? Again...

"Approachable," she said.

He laughed again. "But don't you see? I've been trying to be the opposite."

"Are you?" She looked up at him. "Because you haven't been that way with me."

He rubbed the side of his thumb across her cheek. "That's because—"

The bathroom door opened and Sam came out and headed toward them.

Des ached to pull her into his arms and drag her upstairs to the bedroom, but that would have to wait. "You two ready for some mean grilled cheese sandwiches?"

"Mean ones?" Her brow wrinkled.

He nodded. "The only kind I make. I hope you two can handle them."

"Considering I have a mean appetite, I think I can handle your wimpy grilled cheese."

"Wimpy?" He winked at Sam. "You are going to eat those words, Ms. Pierce."

"Gee, and I thought I was going to eat the sandwiches."

He gave her a look and she laughed, putting her arm through his as they went back toward the kitchen. "I love your dining room." Her head swiveled around to take in the empty, beige-painted room. "What's the style called?"

He rubbed his chin. "I think the proper term is *minimalist*."

She laughed and hugged his arm closer to her side before letting go. Even after she released him, he felt the warmth of her body against his arm. And in the heart he'd been so convinced was stone cold.

Chapter Six

Shadow lifted his head when Natalie pushed the door to Sam's room open even wider, but the cat didn't move from his spot, curled up next to her son. Not that she could blame him; the old furnace was working overtime trying to keep the place warm. She tucked the covers around Sam and ran her hand over his hair. They'd had such a good time that afternoon, picking out a tree. Today, she'd felt as though she were part of a family again, something she'd missed since Ryan's death. She and Sam had both blossomed under Des's attention. Did Des feel the same way? Or would he run as fast as he could if he knew her thoughts?

Her cell phone vibrated and she pulled it out of the pocket of her bathrobe. *Des*. She smiled and left the room before answering. "Hey, everything okay?"

"Yeah, I wanted to say good-night."

Say good-night? Hadn't they done that when they'd left his place? "Oh. Okay."

"I hope you and Sam had fun picking out a tree."

She smiled. "I should be asking you about that. I hope your leg isn't bothering you after tramping around the woods today."

"I'm good. How's Sam?"

She glanced at Sam. "He's out like a light."

"I'm glad he had fun. How about you? I hope you enjoyed yourself, too."

She smiled even though she knew he couldn't see her face. Maybe it would show in her voice. "I did. Thank you for helping us pick out the tree and chopping it down for us."

"I should let you go. Good night and be sure to let me know when you're ready for me to bring the tree over."

"I will. Good night, Des."

She was still smiling when she hung up. She wouldn't have pegged him for late-night, sleepy-voice calls. But then, he was continuing to surprise her. All in a good way.

Natalie spread white frosting on the edges and put the last gingerbread piece in place. She held the pieces together, waiting for the icing to set. She pulled her hand away, stepping back to admire her work. Sam was going to love it. It had been two days since they'd picked out their tree and she wasn't going to be able to hold Sam off much longer. At least the evergreen was fresh enough she wouldn't have to worry about bare branches come Christmas morning.

She wanted Christmas in their new home to be perfect. She wanted to believe that moving to Loon Lake had been the right thing to do. Even if she'd sold the duplex, the proceeds wouldn't have covered buying a similarly sized home in Nashville. Plus, she knew in her heart when she'd visited Loon Lake that she'd found home. Being uprooted hadn't been easy for Sam, but he was settling in and she'd promised him Santa would find him in their new home. She hadn't been able to prevent what had happened to him or the loss of his father, but she was determined to do the things that were in her power. Like having a perfect Christmas.

With Des having the horses at his place, they'd been able to cobble together some hippotherapy sessions for established clients. Des had even been good-natured about putting up with it. Of course, *amiable* was a relative term when it came to Des Gallagher.

Stepping back, she wiped her hands on a dish towel. As she turned to hang the towel back on the oven door handle, a black-and-silver blur raced past her, heading toward the table: the table where she'd left the gingerbread house.

"No!" Natalie yelled and simultaneously lunged for the kitten.

She managed to grab Shadow before he could jump on the table, but in doing so her foot hit the table leg, knocking over the bottle of water she'd set there. It swayed then toppled over onto the completed house, smashing through the back half. Part of the back wall was gone and there was a hole in the roof.

Setting Shadow on the floor, she shooed him away. Why did he have to pick today to try mastering jumping high enough to get onto the kitchen table? Natalie swore, using phrases that would've made her drill-sergeant dad proud. Not that the swearing helped with anything, except maybe her blood pressure, for letting off steam.

Her cell rang and she checked the screen. She inhaled and answered. "Hey."

"What's wrong?"

"What?" She frowned at the phone. Was Des psychic? "What makes you think something is wrong?"

"I can hear it in your voice."

"You can?" His perception made her stomach do a funny little flip-flop.

"Yeah, your voice doesn't have that usual—" he cleared his throat "—sparkle."

She smiled despite what had happened. "You really are an enigma."

"And just yesterday I'd graduated to mysterious." He chuckled. "Quit trying to distract me. I want to know what's wrong."

He was going to think she was silly for being so upset over a house made from cookies. She sighed. "It's my house. One of my walls collapsed and—"

"What?" There was a short pause followed by some of the same words she'd used. "Are you okay? Were you hurt?"

"Hurt? No, I'm mad abou— Oh! You thought I meant my real house. No. No. It was the gingerbread house I was making. I was going to surprise Sam when he got home and now it's ruined."

He swore again. "A gingerbread house? You mean you gave me a heart attack over a cookie house?"

"See? I knew you were going to think I was silly." Damn. Why did she tell him. He was going to think she was nuts. And maybe she was, but the picture-perfect house was now in ruins.

He exhaled. "I never called you silly. I was upset thinking you could have been in a situation where you might have gotten hurt, that's all."

"Sorry. I didn't mean to upset you. And I didn't mean to mislead you. I was making this elaborate house and it was almost finished. I was waiting for the cement to harden and—"

"Hold up. By cement you mean…"

"Sorry. It's icing—you know, like frosting—but it hadn't set yet and the cat tried to jump on the table and well, long story short, half the house is in ruins. The pieces broke and part of it is nothing but rubble. Looks like some sort of earthquake or natural disaster took out half the house."

"I'm sorry."

"Thanks, but I guess it will work out for you and Sam since you'll be able to eat the pieces."

He snorted. "Yeah, like I need to eat more baked goods."

"I had promised Sam I'd have it ready when he got home. Mary Wilson took a couple of the kids to a matinee." She looked at the gingerbread again and grimaced. "Even if I try to get the pieces patched together, a chunk of the roof will be gone and a hunk of one of the walls."

"And that's bad?"

"If you saw this mess, you wouldn't have to ask." She sighed, but was surprised he hadn't brushed off her concerns. Another point in Des's favor. They were adding up fast.

"It might not be a mess to a five-year-old boy."

"Yeah, right."

"Have you ever been a five-year-old boy?"

She grinned. "Okay. I see your point, but it makes it hard to decorate."

"You were going to decorate it?"

"I had planned to let Sam help me." She shooed the curious cat away from the table.

"How do you decorate a cookie house?"

"With gumdrops, candy canes, stuff like that." She glanced at the ingredients she'd laid out on the counter with high hopes.

"Where's the house now?"

"It's still on the kitchen table. Why?"

"Can you patch the bigger pieces together?"

"Yeah, but why would I want to?"

"Do it. I have an idea. I'll be right over."

"Are you some sort of gingerbread house whisperer?" she asked.

"Something like that. Patch together what you can and then leave it. Don't get rid of it. Promise?"

"I promise." She was still confused but decided to go along with it if this meant Des was coming over.

After she patched together what pieces of gingerbread she could, she raced into her bedroom to change. Rolling her eyes at herself in the mirror, Natalie brushed her hair and applied lip gloss. *Eager much?* she asked her reflection as her doorbell rang. She smoothed her festive sweater over her jeans with shaky hands. When was the last time she'd experienced these heady sensations? The breathless anticipation, the racing pulse, the grin that wouldn't quit? She'd been a college freshman getting ready for a first date with that cute senior, Ryan Pierce.

Des waited for her to answer the door, hoping his idea would work. If not, he was going to look like a fool.

The door opened and Natalie greeted him. For a moment he stood speechless. She was smiling at him, her lips shiny and begging to be kissed. He ached to lean over and kiss her until they were both breathless and—

"Des? Is something wrong?" She peered at him.

Recovering, he quirked an eyebrow. "You didn't tell me this was Ugly Sweater Day."

"What?" She glanced down at her herself. "I…"

He laughed and gave her a chaste, no-tongue kiss— unlike the messy one he'd been craving—before stepping inside. "I'm joking."

She narrowed her eyes but her smile stayed in place. "Joking? Or trying to save your hide?"

"I confess I've grown attached to my hide. It's been with me for thirty-four years now. I'd hate to lose it over a googly-eyed reindeer with a red pompom nose."

"So we're in agreement my sweater is kitschy and not ugly?"

"Yes, ma'am."

She swatted his shoulder. "What's in the bag? Did you bring replacement gingerbread?"

"Call me Mr. Fix-It." He pulled away when she tried to reach for the bag. "Show me to this disaster house."

"Disaster is right, but unless you have replacement gingerbread it's a lost cause."

He cupped her cheek in his free hand. "Let me be the judge of that."

She pressed her face against his palm. "It's in the kitchen, what's left of it. The house, not the kitchen."

He chuckled. "I guessed that much."

"I wanted to be sure to clarify. I don't want you having any more heart attacks."

"I like a woman who's concerned for my health." He couldn't resist and gave her a kiss. His lips lingered but he force himself to keep it light or he might not be able to stop.

Following her farther into the house, he licked his lips. Peppermint. He'd never again taste or smell peppermint and not think of Natalie.

In the kitchen, she pointed to the gingerbread like Vanna White revealing a vowel. He stood in front of what was left of the confectionery disaster and studied it. "I'm impressed."

She snorted a laugh. "Is that good or bad impressed?"

Straightening up, he cleared his throat. "Just impressed."

He opened the bag and pulled out the die-cast airplane that sat atop the dresser in his bedroom. He held up the jet. "Naval aviation to the rescue."

"Oh."

He frowned. "What's wrong?"

"That looks much too expensive for a five-year-old boy." She shook her head. "Granted, Sam will be disappointed by the ruined gingerbread house, but I don't think we need to bribe him. He'll get over it."

"Oh, ye of little faith." He studied the mess and then

strategically set the plane so it appeared the jet had crashed into the house.

"Oh, wow," Natalie said. Grateful as she was for Des coming to her rescue, her feelings went much deeper than gratitude. And they were turning into something more. Much, much more. Those emotions elicited as much fear as they did excitement. And had nothing to do with gingerbread houses.

Before she could say anything else, Sam burst through the side door from the carport.

A dark-haired woman appeared in the doorway and waved. "Hey, I wanted to let you know we had a great time with Sam, but Elliott's asleep in his car seat so I can't come in," she said, even as she glanced toward the driveway. "And I see you have company anyway so I'll call you later and we can catch up. Wow, clever gingerbread house. Oh, hi, Des. Sorry, but I don't want to leave Elliott alone with the car running."

"Thanks, Mary." Natalie shut the door after the woman dashed off and turned back. "That whirlwind was Brody Wilson's wife, Mary. She recognized you, so I'm assuming you've met her before. She took a group of the kids to see that new Christmas movie and included Sam."

Sam stood staring at the gingerbread house with the tail end of the plane sticking out. She smiled at Des and put her hands on Sam's shoulders. "As you can see, there was a little accident."

Sam shook his head and ran off down the hall toward his room. Des met her gaze and his gut clenched. He'd hoped to save Natalie's project but should've known he was no one's hero.

"Well, at least you tried and I appreciate it. I'm sure Sam will…" She trailed off when her son came running back into the kitchen, the cat following on his heels. He held up a miniature fire truck and set it next to the house along with a toy police car.

Natalie choked out what sounded like a mixture of a laugh and a sob. Sam pulled something out of his pocket and placed LEGO people around the scene, his tongue in the corner of his mouth as he concentrated on his work.

"That's exactly what it needed," Des said and nodded his approval when Sam looked up to him. "Great job, bud."

The look on Sam's face was priceless. Des had trouble swallowing past the frog in his throat. Who knew something so simple could mean so much? He met Natalie's gaze and fought the feelings tightening his chest. He supposed he'd accomplished a lot of things in his life to be proud of, but being responsible for that expression on Sam's face topped the list. Who would have thought a five-year-old with a gingerbread house could mean so much to him?

Sam opened and closed his mouth, stamped his foot and ran again toward his room with the cat scampering after him.

Natalie pulled out a chair and sank down. "I can't imagine what it must be like not to be able to express myself using words."

"Have you tried sign language?" Des pulled out a chair and sat next to her. He reached over and took her hand in his. It had been a long time since he'd tried to comfort anyone and he wasn't even sure if his attempts would be welcome, but he had to try.

"Yeah, we—"

Sam appeared once again in the kitchen with his tablet. He tapped a picture and a computerized voice said, "Love" and Sam pointed to the gingerbread house. He tapped again and the voice said, "Thank you."

"You're welcome, bud."

Natalie wiped her cheeks with the backs of her hands and jumped up. "Let's get your jacket off."

While Natalie was hanging it up, Des got up and went to the counter. "Are these candies what you were going to use to decorate?"

She came to stand next to him. "Yeah, but gumdrops and candy canes hardly seem appropriate now."

"I guess Sam and I hijacked your Christmas house." He rubbed his knuckles across her back.

"I might be able to get into the spirit." She opened a cupboard, rummaged around and pulled out a food coloring set and held it up.

"What can you do with that?"

"I can color the icing and use it to enhance your scene with some flames."

Sam held up his tablet again. The computer voice repeated, "Love."

She sighed. "Not what I had in mind this morning when I was making the pieces for the house, but don't let anyone say I can't go with the flow."

"That's getting into the spirit of things." Des squeezed her shoulder.

"Says the man who hates Christmas."

He leaned close and kissed her temple before straightening up and taking a step back. Was she changing his mind about Christmas by replacing bad memories with good ones?

She cleared her throat. "So what are we calling this?"

He put his hand under his chin as he studied the house. "How about we call it a simulated disaster scenario?"

"Simulated?" She raised her eyebrows.

Sam jumped up and down and tugged on her sleeve, nodding his head.

"Okay, I'm outnumbered. Simulated disaster scenario it is. Now, let's get this decorated and find someplace to put it where the cat can't reach it or the disaster won't be simulated."

She mixed up some red and orange icing and put it into pastry decorating bags. Des picked up Sam and held him over the house so he could decorate with less chance of bumping into the building. Sam took his time and piped icing flames on with a precision Des admired.

After Sam finished, Des lowered him to the floor and put up his palm. Sam gave him a high five and giggled.

"Great job, sport." Des wondered if Sam would someday find solace and satisfaction in creativity as he had. Sam might enjoy making a simple stained glass item. Maybe he'd suggest it sometime and if Sam was interested, he'd teach him what to do.

Natalie found some black coloring she'd had left over from Halloween and they used it on some of the bigger broken pieces to make them look charred from the fire. She'd been quick to switch gears from her original vision for the cookie house. What would his life have looked like if he'd a more structured family life growing up? He pushed the thought aside. He could only go forward, not back.

Natalie stood back and admired their work. "I think it needs one more touch."

Des turned to Sam but the boy shrugged and shook his head.

"To look like soot," she explained as she sprinkled cinnamon over it.

Once it was all finished, Des helped her carry the house and the cardboard square she'd built it on into Sam's bedroom. They set it on top of a tall dresser after deciding the cat hadn't mastered leaping that high. Natalie turned on the small light located on the dresser to illuminate the scene.

Sam stayed in his room so he could admire the gingerbread creation. Natalie walked down the hall with Des. "Thank you for this. I can't tell you how much this whole thing has meant to me. And I feel as though we crossed a hurdle when he went and got his tablet. In the past, I've had to give the iPad to him and ask him to use it."

Des squeezed her hand. "Maybe he wasn't ready."

She heaved a sigh. "I've been torn between letting him develop at his own pace and giving him the support and encouragement he needs."

He glanced down the hall to be sure Sam was still in his room before taking her in his arms. "I'd say continue to do what you have been."

"Thanks." She reached up, cupped his face.

"Glad I could help." He let her go when she pulled away. "I need to get back home. I want to get the horses into the barn and get the plow ready to attach to my truck. If the weather forecast is correct, I'm going to need to attach it soon."

"Finally, our first snow," she said and laughed when he rolled his eyes.

"We'll see how you feel about it this time tomorrow."

She stuck her chin out. "You know you don't scare me. Even that first day when you were so rude."

"Was I rude?"

"Yes, very," she said but her grin gave her away. "But I knew you were all bark, no bite."

"And how did you know that?" He was glad he hadn't scared her away for good. He couldn't imagine not getting to know her.

"I'm a good judge of character. Besides, you winked at Sam."

He clicked his tongue. "Was that my mistake?"

She patted his chest. "Told you I was a good judge of character."

He threw his head back. "Then you should be running for the hills."

"Nah, I like what I see, Des Gallagher."

"And I'm grateful you do."

Natalie put her hand on Sam's shoulder as they stood in the doorway and watched Des climb out of his truck. After yesterday's fun with the gingerbread house, she felt as though their relationship had entered a new phase. He waved to them hefting the evergreen from the pickup's bed, then limping up the sidewalk with the tree.

Natalie winced at his motion. She hated that Des was so often in pain from his leg. She had yet to learn what had happened. Several times she'd been tempted to come right out and ask but wasn't quite comfortable enough yet to do so. She didn't want him thinking his limp bothered her by pointing it out. His gait was simply a part of him, like his coal-black hair or brown eyes, and she was attracted to the whole package. Yes, she liked all of him. A whole lot.

Sam hovered excitedly as Des carried the tree into the house.

Des held the evergreen to the side so he could see Sam. "Hey, there, bud. Ready to get this set up?"

Sam clapped and nodded.

Natalie brought out a box of ornaments from the closet. Her mother had given her many of the ornaments they'd used on trees from her childhood after her dad had died. She also had some she and Ryan had collected during their short marriage. Before bringing out the box, she'd removed one that had celebrated their wedding anniversary. But she'd kept the ones Ryan had bought for her celebrating other occasions. Removing reminders of Ryan had not been her intention. His daddy might be gone but his memory needed to be kept alive for Sam, even if it was time for her to move forward. Starting a new relationship didn't erase the past and she'd have to learn how to integrate the two for Sam's sake. She had a few new ones she'd bought at the church's Christmas in July bazaar to signify their fresh start in Loon Lake. So there was a mix of old and new, past and present.

Des got the tree situated in the stand she had put in front of the window. He secured the trunk and she added water.

"We'll string the lights first," Des said as he opened one of the new boxes of lights she'd set on the couch.

"Wait. There's one thing I need to do before that," she said as she set up the folding step stool next to the tree. She got on the top step with her precut pieces of twine.

"What are you doing?" Des put his hands on his hips as he watched her.

"Cat-proofing the tree." She tied the twine around the trunk under the top branches and strung it over the curtain rod. "At least it won't tip over."

"Where is the cat?" Des asked and put his hand under her elbow as she started to climb off the stool; his hand lingered for a few extra seconds after she'd stepped off. Heat flared where his skin had all too briefly touched hers. It made her think of them being together...and alone...

Her heart beat so fast it threatened to jump out of her chest as she continued to gaze at him. She leaned closer and— Sam shifted, reminding her they weren't alone. As much as she might wish it.

"I shut Shadow in Sam's bedroom until I had the tree secured since I didn't know what his reaction would be. You can go let him out now, Sam."

As soon as Sam left to go get the cat, Des pulled her close for a kiss. Their lips met in a heady rush, too rushed and hard to be labeled tender, but whatever tenderness their kiss lacked, it made up for in enthusiasm. A door opened and they pulled apart, both breathing hard.

"Mmm." She licked her lips. "What was that for?"

He shrugged, his gaze on her lips. "Couldn't help myself."

"I'm glad you have no self-control." She gave him a quick peck as footsteps came down the hall. "Me, either."

Before they could do anything else, Sam came back with the cat close behind.

"Here." She handed Sam a piece of paper.

Sam crinkled the paper into a ball and immediately had the cat's attention. He tossed the paper, and the kitten skittered after it, batting it around the room.

"Wow. Do you have a special technique for doing that? Or are you like some cat expert?" Des asked Sam, who rolled his eyes. Des playfully poked his side until Sam was giggling.

Natalie's heart melted as Des interacted with Sam. She couldn't have asked for anything more for her son this Christmas. No matter what the future held, she and Sam would have wonderful memories of their first Christmas in Loon Lake. She knew from experience that difficult memories had a way of bringing the sweetest joy as time mellowed pain.

Still, a ripple of unease coursed through her. What would happen to Sam if Des reverted to his old ways of shutting people out? How would she explain it to Sam? Could she?

She shouldn't let her fears of something that hadn't happened, and might never happen, spoil the here and now, so she shook off the melancholy thoughts as best she could.

By the time Des strung the lights to his satisfaction, Natalie had noticed he was a bit of a perfectionist. They divided up the task of putting the ornaments on the tree.

Des put the ones on the higher branches, Natalie the middle and Sam the lowest.

"Ready to put the star on top, bud?" Des asked after the last ornament was in place.

Des picked up Sam so he could put the star on top of the decorated tree. After setting Sam down, Des plugged the star into a socket on the end of the lights he'd strung.

He stepped back and turned to them. "Are we ready for the tree-lighting ceremony?"

"Ceremony?" Natalie turned to Sam, who lifted his shoulders and held his hands out, palms up in a "me either" gesture.

"Like the town tree. You're not the mayor, but I thought you might like to say a few words," Des said.

She laughed. "I'll pass, but thanks."

"Okay. Why don't we let Sam flip the switch? That okay with you, bud?"

Sam nodded and Des held up the power strip he'd brought with him to plug the lights into. Sam pressed the on switch and the less-than-desirable tree took on a happy glow.

Natalie's heart lit up as brightly as the tree. The three of them—together—made her imagine things beyond this Christmas, things she had no place imagining.

"I saw how fascinated he was with what they did at the town tree-lighting." He shrugged. "I also wasn't sure how many outlets you had since this is an older home."

"Well, I appreciate it and I'm sure Sam does, too." She wasn't just falling in love with Des. Despite her concerns over the future, she was all the way—madly, deeply, hopelessly—in love. A scary prospect, because she didn't know what had caused Des to shut himself away from the world. She suspected whatever scars he had ran deep and many had never been healed.

She glanced at Sam, who was watching Des with what amounted to hero-worship. Yeah, she wasn't the only one who'd fallen under his spell.

"I made lasagna earlier today and I hope you'll join us for supper." She realized how much she wanted him to say yes. Tonight and forever.

He lifted his face and sniffed. "Is that what that delicious smell is?"

Silly, but that simple comment made her stomach flutter. "Yeah, it's one of Sam's favorites."

"Well, after those pancakes, I trust his judgment. Not to mention I haven't had a home-cooked meal in a while."

She frowned, feeling both happy to be feeding him and sad that he had no one to cook for him. To *care* for him. "How long is a while?"

He shrugged but had a strangely impassive expression as if afraid of revealing something he didn't want her to see.

She let it drop. "So no pressure to impress?"

"You've already blown me away with your cookies and other goodies."

"So my cookies appeal to you?"

"That's not all I find appealing," he whispered and waggled his eyebrows.

A delicious tingle ran down her spine and lifted the hairs on her arms at his words. Did this mean he was feeling the same intense feelings that she was? Before she could say anything more, Sam approached Des and tugged on his sleeve.

Des leaned down. "What you need, Sam, my man?"

Sam pressed his tablet. "Love. Tree. Thanks."

"Did you find 'tree' on there?" Des asked and pointed to the tablet.

Sam grinned and nodded.

"Great job. Put her there, bud." Des held out his hand palm up. After Sam gave him a palm slap, Des turned to her. "I'll be happy to help in the kitchen, but first, I have one more thing for the tree."

"Oh?" What more could he have? He'd already done so much for them.

"Yeah, it's in my truck. Let me go get it." He held up his hand as if to halt any questions. "It's a surprise."

She felt like a kid herself as they waited for Des, who came back in with a slim rectangular package. Setting it down, he pulled a small folded knife from his pocket and unsealed the box to reveal a model train and track.

"To go around the tree," Des explained.

"How wonderful," she said, but her voice sounded strangled.

Fearing she might embarrass herself, not to mention Sam and Des, she headed for the kitchen. Bursting into tears would be a bit difficult to explain. How could she explain something she didn't understand? Because as much as she might want to, she didn't have the words to express her gratitude. She couldn't imagine a better father figure for Sam. Des was in the running for World's Best Dad. "Let me go set the table and fix a salad to go with the lasagna."

In the kitchen she wiped her face, listening to Des

talking to Sam as they set up the track for the train. Every so often she heard Sam's iPad talking. Maybe Des had been right that Sam hadn't been ready until now to use it. Or maybe his relationship with Des had prompted him to use it. Whatever the reason, she felt like rejoicing this new milestone—along with celebrating *her* own, newfound bond with Des.

In those dark days following Ryan's death, falling in love again had never occurred to her. Then as she healed, she doubted she might ever find anyone special enough again. Now the possibilities that lay ahead of them were all she thought of.

Chapter Seven

After getting the train set up and working, Des took a few minutes to share in Sam's enjoyment. Although he felt guilty for choosing to put together the train for Sam before going into the kitchen, he suspected Natalie had wanted a few moments alone. After catching her surreptitiously wiping tears away, he let her escape.

Not that he could blame her. He'd been grappling with his feelings because Sam was such a large part of this relationship. At five years older, Patrick had been the only father figure he'd known in his life. Each time he was with Sam, Des channeled his early memories of his big brother helping him, guiding him and having fun.

He stopped in the doorway to the kitchen. Natalie was bending over in tight jeans as she pulled a large pan from the oven, her long hair tied back with a bright tie. He wanted to release her hair and let those silky strands slide through his fingers. When she stood, her face was flushed from the heat of the oven. That flush reminded him of when he'd kissed her, making him want to do it all over again. And again.

He would forevermore consider cookies an aphrodisiac. She looked at home in her kitchen and he knew she tasted sweeter than any cookie she baked. Longing for her sweetness, he yearned to be at home here with her.

"Hey." She set the pan on the counter and pulled off the oven mitts. "Got the train all set up?"

"Come and see it." He held out his hand, hoping she'd take it. She did, and his heart swelled to a size he hadn't known it could occupy in his chest.

They stood in the doorway, the lights from the tree reflected in her eyes. His heart squeezed in his chest. God, she was beautiful.

"You were right," she whispered, turning her face toward him.

"I'm sorry, but could you be more specific?" he whispered back. She narrowed her eyes at him and he touched her chin. "I'm right about so many things."

She rolled her eyes and elbowed him. "I was talking about the tree. It's beautiful…in its own unique way."

He put his arm around her and pulled her closer. "Are you saying you doubted me?"

"I shouldn't have." She pushed out her lower lip. "I'll know better next time."

He gave her a mock scowl. "See that you do."

Sam made a noise and they jumped apart and turned toward him. The cat had caused a train derailment.

"Uh-oh, bud, simulated train disaster?" he asked and Sam giggled.

"Hey, don't go giving him any ideas," she warned, but her lips curved into a smile.

Damn. With only his older brother as an example, he knew his skills as a dad were sorely lacking. Trial and error might work for some things, but not so much when it came to parenting. He sighed. "Maybe the train wasn't such a good idea."

She shook her head. "I'm sure I'll figure something out."

"It doesn't bother you?" His mother would never have stood for any of this. She'd complain he was making a mess that she would have to clean up, despite the fact that he always picked up after himself.

"It's not the end of the world," Natalie was saying. She squared her shoulders and continued, "What will be a disaster—and not the simulated kind—is if my lasagna gets cold. Sam, put Shadow in your bedroom for now."

Sam laughed, picked up the cat and cuddled it as he went down the hall.

Des turned to her and quirked an eyebrow. "Hmm, did you say your father was a drill sergeant in the army?"

She scrunched her face. "Too harsh?"

Des burst out laughing. "Oh, yeah, I could see both of them quaking in their boots."

"What about you? Are you quaking in your boots?"

"You better know it."

"Good. Now march to the table and eat." She turned on her heel and went into the kitchen.

She walked away, her hips swaying in a way that had him groaning, even though he suspected she was exaggerating the movement. Damn, but she was beautiful coming and going. He was getting in deeper and deeper. And loving every minute of it.

Sam came back and Des put his arm around his shoulders. "C'mon, bud, we better get in there before supper gets cold."

After supper he helped her clean up the kitchen. Even mundane chores took on a new meaning when he shared them with her.

"How about we go out front to see how the tree looks from the street," he suggested after they'd loaded the dishwasher and wiped down the counter.

"I love that idea. Maybe we can walk a bit down the street and look at some of the others. A few people have lights strung along their bushes and some of those lit-up deer on their lawns." Her smile turned to a frown. "It won't bother your leg, will it?"

"I'm not an invalid," he snapped, but regretted his churlish tone when distress marred her features. Hurting Natalie was the last thing he wanted, so he made an effort to soften his tone. "I'll be fine."

She opened her mouth to say something, but after glancing at Sam, she nodded.

Des touched her arm and raised his brows in a silent appeal for forgiveness. When she smiled, he released his breath and dropped his hand.

"Ready to go, sport?" he asked, resting his hand on Sam's shoulder.

Sam grinned and gave him a double thumbs up.

He laughed. "I'll take that as a 'heck yeah.'"

They all bundled up and went out into the cold.

"The tree looks so pretty," Natalie said as she stood looking at the house.

"You sound surprised," he grumbled and when she laughed, he flicked the end of her nose.

Sam looked up at Des and pointed down the street.

"I think he wants to check out the competition," Natalie said.

Des nodded. "I think you're right. Shall we?"

Sam went ahead and Des used the opportunity to hold Natalie's hand as they strolled to the end of her cul-de-sac. His leg was sore but the slow pace suited him. Holding Natalie's hand felt too good to worry about the aches and pains he lived with every day.

A car drove past and the driver tooted the horn and waved. As Des returned the friendly greeting, he realized how much his life had changed in the short time he'd known Natalie and Sam. He was doing things he wouldn't have contemplated a month ago, thinking things he wouldn't have even thought of and wanting things he hadn't in a long, long time.

When they got back to the duplex, they admired the tree from the street again. Des clapped Sam on the shoulder. "I declare Sam to be the best Christmas tree picker-outer in Loon Lake."

Back in the house, Natalie told Sam it was time to brush his teeth and get ready for bed.

After Sam went down the hall, she turned to him with an expectant expression. "I hope you'll stay after Sam goes to bed."

Des gave himself a mental high five. Clearing his

throat, he tried to keep the excitement from his voice. "I'd like that."

"Me, too. I'll be right back." She started to walk away but turned back to check on him as if afraid he might make a run for it when her back was turned.

He grinned at the notion and settled on the sofa and put his socked feet on the coffee table.

She frowned and took a step back toward him.

He removed his feet. "Sorry. Is that not allowed?"

"No. No, it's okay to put your feet up. Please." She waved her hand in a helpless gesture. "Is your leg bothering you? I shouldn't have made you walk around the neighborhood in the cold and—"

"As much as I appreciate your concern, I am well acquainted with the word *no.*" He forced a laugh. "And I frequently use it when it suits me."

"Of course. I…" Her face red, she gnawed on her bottom lip.

What the hell was wrong with him? He didn't want to fight with her, and not over something so trivial. He got up and went to her, doing his best to disguise his limp. He cupped her cheek. "I'm fine."

When she looked skeptical, he turned her around and gave a gentle shove. "Go. Do what you have to. I'll be right here."

She glanced over her shoulder.

He grinned. "Actually, I'll be over there on the couch."

She started back down the hall and called over her shoulder, "Put your feet up, Lieutenant. That's an order."

"Oh, believe me, I intend to, but tell me something."

She stopped and turned. "Yes?"

"Do you plan on being this bossy later?" He quirked an eyebrow and studied her from across the room.

Her eyes widened and a blush spread across her face. "I guess you'll have to wait and see."

She turned and hurried down the hall before he could respond. Instead of chafing at being bossed around and fussed over, following her commands didn't leave him feeling defensive. Huh, maybe the promise of things to come made a difference.

Chuckling, he went back to the couch and put his feet up. He had to admit it did ease the ache a bit.

She came back a few minutes later with Sam and the cat following close on their heels. "He wants to say good-night."

Sam stuck out his hand and Des shook his hand, then pulled him closer and gave him a hug, which Sam returned.

"C'mon, Sam, I think Shadow wants to go to bed."

Sam giggled and picked up the cat.

His chest tightened as Natalie and Sam walked with the cat back down the hall. What would it be like to be a part of this ritual every night? To belong to something like this, to belong in Natalie's world…forever?

"Did you want to watch a movie?" she asked when she came back into the living room and sat next to him on the sofa. "I promise to stay awake this time."

He had more on his mind than that, but he'd take any excuse to linger. If that meant watching a movie—even one of her dreaded Christmas romances—he'd take it. Putting his arm over the back of the couch, Des toyed with the hair falling over her shoulder. "If that's what you want."

She began to fidget, pulling at the neck of her shirt. "To be honest, I'd rather we uh…uh…" She blushed. "Geez, I'm an enlightened and empowered twenty-first-century woman, so this shouldn't be hard, but it is. And so, so awkward."

Relief rippled through him along with a sexual thrill. Were they on the same page? Looked like his self-imposed period of celibacy was over. He opened his mouth, then realized he didn't have any protection with him. Ha! He didn't have any at his house, either. Damn. "I would love to, but I don't have any—"

"I do," she interrupted in a rush.

"You what?" His heart thudded in his chest. Could she mean what he thought—hoped—she meant…

"I have some." This time her face blossomed scarlet. "When I was in Boston… I…I…well, I figured no one would know me there so…"

"Wait…" He put his thumb under her chin and lifted her head. "Didn't you go to Boston after our third meeting?"

She scowled. "Now you're assuming I bought them because of you."

"Well, I…" *Guilty.* He had made that very assumption.

She poked him. "Of course they're because of you."

He couldn't see his own face, but he was certain he had a silly grin plastered all over it. Pulling her into his arms, he bent to kiss her, but before his lips touched hers he whispered, "We are talking condoms, right?"

"We are. Now kiss me." She sighed and melted against him, their lips meeting.

He cradled her face in his palms and kissed her as

if he'd been waiting for her his entire life. And perhaps he had. Strands of her silky hair caught on the rough skin of his fingers, her lavender scent tickling and inciting his senses.

He'd been with other women and even engaged, but he'd never felt like this before. All his nerve endings were electrified to the point where he expected sparks where their bodies touched.

He left her mouth to kiss his way across her cheek to beneath her ear and then the spot where her neck met her shoulder.

She groaned. "I had a dream about you last night."

"Mmm...tell me more about this dream." He nibbled on her earlobe.

"You'll think it was silly." She ran her fingernails lightly up and down his back.

"Tell me anyway," he urged.

She sighed. "You were wearing dress whites and swept me off my feet."

He groaned. How often had he heard that before? "Are you sure you weren't dreaming about Richard Gere?"

She shook her head. "Who?"

He searched her face but still couldn't be sure if she was serious or not. "*An Officer and a Gentleman*. The movie."

She smiled. "Sorry. That was before my time."

"Mine, too." He found it hard to believe she wasn't referring to that movie. Ashley had talked about that scene, as had other women he'd met.

He wished he could make her dream a reality, but he

also knew his limitations. His days of sweeping women off their feet were over.

That had never bothered him as much as it did now, because he wanted to make Natalie's dreams come true...no matter how hokey or cliché. "If I had Richard Gere's sturdy legs, I'd sweep you off your feet and carry you anywhere you desired. Since I don't, how about I take your hand and lead you to the bedroom instead?"

She placed her palm against his cheek. He leaned into her touch, yearning for that connection with her.

"Sounds like a good plan. I'm capable of walking. Why risk injury before the fun begins?"

He brushed the hair back from her face. There was a vulnerability about this woman that awakened his protective instincts. "If I could make your dreams come true, I would."

She lifted her hand and pressed it to her lips, then pressed her fingers to his lips. The gesture was chaste and at the same time so sensual he experienced her touch all the way to his toes.

What he could or couldn't do didn't seem to bother Natalie. She accepted him the way he was and didn't prattle on about how it was too bad he couldn't fly jets any longer. Was it because she hadn't known him before? Or that she liked living in Loon Lake and wouldn't feel as though she'd been cheated out of something she'd expected from him? Something deep inside shifted around the region of his heart.

Tingling all over, Natalie led Des to her bedroom. Mindful of her son, she locked the door. A lit lamp was casting a warm glow over the bed.

Suddenly shy, her hands shook as she pulled out the

box of condoms from the top drawer. Biting her bottom lip, she set it on the bedside table.

Des choked out a laugh and picked up the box, turning it over in his hands. "Did you get a volume discount?"

"It's been a while and…" She was about to get intimate with this man—at least that was the plan. And yet she didn't want to tell him there'd been no one in the past three years.

He set the box back down and positioned himself in front of her. "Making up for lost time?"

What must he think of her? Why hadn't she taken out a few condoms? "Look, if you—"

He pressed his fingers against her lips. "I'm sorry for teasing. I guess I'm a bit nervous."

Her eyes widened. "Guys get nervous, too?"

He coaxed her into his arms. "This one does when he's with a woman as beautiful as you and when it's been as long as it has."

She blushed. He thought she was beautiful. She rubbed her cheek against the soft cotton of his shirt. He smelled of woodsmoke, pine and fabric softener. "Are you telling me that it's been a while since you…?"

"Don't look so surprised. You've seen where I live and how I treat unexpected visitors." He chuckled.

The vibrations from his deep voice against her cheek raised the hairs on her arm and sent a delicious chill through her. She lifted her face to his. "You were a bit of a grizzly, but in your defense I did barge in. I'm still not sure where I got the courage to do that."

"I tried to scare you off by acting like a jerk, but it didn't work." He shifted, fitting her against him.

She ran her hands up and down his back, her finger-nails scraping him.

"Maybe I'm able to see past that gruff exterior to what's underneath." She placed her palm over his chest. "I see what's in here."

"Ah, X-ray vision. Good thing I put on clean under-wear every day."

"See? I knew there was a sense of humor under there." Any misgivings she may have had vanished. She wanted him and she wanted this. Ached for his touch, his and no one else's.

His eyes darkened as if he'd recognized her desire. "The homemade candy and cookies were a stroke of genius. Did you know I had a sweet tooth? Is that why you brought the candy?" Although it was an innocuous question, his voice was husky.

"When I asked about you, Tavie mentioned that you load way too much sugar in your coffee. She says you're trying to offset all that grumpiness." She had trouble concentrating on the conversation because his hands were under her sweater, roaming over bare skin. His callused hands were causing her breathing to become erratic.

"Ah, but I've been told my grumpiness is one of my virtues," he whispered close to her ear.

She shivered. "You're twisting my words, Des Gal-lagher."

Working his shirt free of his pants, she slid her hands underneath the fabric and moaned when her exploring hands encountered chest hair.

He groaned. "I love it when you say my name in that sexy little drawl."

"Des Gallagher," she whispered and made sure to drag it out to as many syllables as she could.

"You're killing me, sweetheart. Now it's my turn to make you plead."

He lifted her sweater and pulled it over her head with a crackle of static electricity. "Sorry," he murmured and tried to tame the silky strands.

"It's okay. It gets like this during the winter. I feel like the bride of Frankenstein."

He twined his fingers in her hair, fisted his hand and gave it a gentle tug. "I've wanted to do that for the longest time."

"And I've imagined you doing just that."

He groaned low in his throat and kissed her. She lost herself in his touch as he eased them toward the bed until the mattress hit the back of her knees. She'd told him the truth about wanting his hands in her hair and all over. She wanted this, wanted him. Now.

She laid on the bed and he followed, never breaking contact with her lips. He moved so they were laying face-to-face and cupped her breasts in his palms. The lace of the bra brushed against her nipples, sending fire shooting to the apex of her thighs. She made a sound in her throat and he squeezed with one hand and reached around with the other and unclasped her bra, freeing her breasts.

He kissed and sucked, driving her into a frenzy of sweet, sweet torture.

"Please," she groaned but had no idea what she was pleading for.

He unsnapped her jeans and eased the zipper down as he rained kisses over her stomach. She helped him by shimmying out of the pants, leaving her in nothing but her new pink lace bikini panties.

He groaned and put his hands on her hips and rubbed his thumbs along the lace.

"So beautiful," he whispered and kissed the skin above the waistband, drawing his tongue across the top.

His touch set her on fire and she felt beautiful, sexy and desired, pregnancy stretch marks included.

She pushed at his shoulders. "You have too many clothes on. I want to touch you."

Des pushed himself off the bed and began stripping off his clothes as eager as a teenager being with a woman for the first time. If he wasn't careful he'd lose control with embarrassing results, especially when her eyes darkened as her gaze traveled to his groin.

His pants around his ankles, he froze when she gasped. His scars. Damn. How could he have forgotten about those? Sick to his stomach, he began yanking the pants back up.

"No. Don't." She scrambled off the bed and kneeled in front of him, tugging the jeans back down.

Her fingers traced the angry marks, then her lips followed where those soothing fingers had been. Until that moment, he'd barely acknowledged their existence because they represented all he'd lost, but looking down at Natalie the bitterness he'd carried began slipping away. They were scars, nothing more, nothing less.

Fearing he might embarrass himself, not by loss of sexual control but by bawling, he put his hands under her arms. He urged her up, cupped his hands around her face and gave her a hard, bruising, and yet somehow cleansing, kiss.

When she made a noise, he broke the contact with their lips but continued to cradle her head in his palms. "Did I hurt you?"

"No, I was right there with you," she whispered, and threaded her fingers in his hair, resuming the kiss.

He wasn't sure who moved first, but they were both back on the bed in a tangle of arms and legs.

"Isn't it about time to lose these?" she asked, inserting her fingers under the waistband of his boxer briefs and pulling.

When he sprang free, she reached over. Her touch was gentle, tentative, but his hips bucked under her hands and he couldn't hold back the groan. Growing bolder, she stroked him and he gritted his teeth to hold on to his control. He attempted to calculate lift-to-drag ratios in his head but his brain had ceased to function, leaving him little more than an incoherent fool.

Leaning down, he took the puckered point of her nipple into his mouth and sucked. She squeezed him in response and he grinned against her skin.

He ran his fingers up and down her side. She arched away, giggling.

"Is my Southern gal ticklish?" he asked and touched her again, triggering the same response.

"Yes, but I'm a Muggle, not a Southern gal."

He laughed. "I have no idea what a Muggle is, but I love hearing you say it."

"It's a person with no magical ability. From the Harry Potter books."

He pressed a kiss to that spot. "I'd say you were pretty magical."

"Bless your heart, aren't you a peach," she said and giggled again.

"I have a feeling that's another one of your insults," he said in a voice that was supposed to be stern but he couldn't pull it off.

"Sorry."

"You can insult me all you want as long as you use that voice."

His wandering fingers found a spot that made her moan and his blood began to pound. Teasing forgotten, he used all his skill to work her into a frenzy.

"Oh, please," she begged. "Yes, right there."

He applied a little more pressure and she came apart in his hand.

He scooted up and grabbed one of the condoms and fumbled until he got it opened.

"May I?" she asked as he started to sheath himself.

What sweet torture. Her hands shook as she rolled the condom in place.

"I can't hold out much longer." He moved over her and spread her thighs. "But you said it's been a while and I don't want to hurt you."

"You won't." She shook her head, her blue eyes dark with pleasure and trust.

She trusts me. He groaned again. "Tell me to stop if it hurts and I will."

He took his time until he was satisfied she was ready for him. He pulled out, then thrust into her. Lifting her legs, she crossed her heels around the small of his back and urged him to keep up his pace. When he got too close he slowed down, trying to wring as much out of both of them as he could. Finally, he couldn't hold off any longer and, using his thumb, he brought her to the peak and made sure she tumbled over again.

Closing his eyes he thrust hard and deep one last time before he exploded in a release that bewildered him. He'd never experienced anything this intense and perhaps if he wasn't so numb with pleasure, he'd be able to figure out why or the implications of what had happened.

He stretched out next to her and anchored her against him with his arm. She rested her head on his chest.

"That was amazing." She caressed his chest. "Was it good for you, too?"

"Amazing," he echoed and kissed the top of her head. "I'm glad my behavior didn't scare you away, Natalie."

"Me, too." She cuddled closer, her fingers drawing swirls on his chest. "You seem like such a loner. Do you have any family?"

Did he want to talk about this? He remembered the look of trust in her eyes. She'd trusted him with her heart—and her body—so the least he could do was offer her the same. "I had a brother."

She lifted her head. "Had?"

He puffed up his cheeks and released the trapped air. "His name was Patrick. He was five years older."

"What happened?" She laid her head back down. "Forget I asked. You don't have to spill your guts because…because of this."

"I know." He laced his fingers through hers. "He committed suicide when he was seventeen…went out in the woods and hung himself."

"I'm so sorry. That must've been terrible for your parents."

"It was just my mother. Technically, he was a half brother. Same mother, different fathers. Patrick's father died of a brain tumor when my brother was a baby. Patrick's father was the one great love of my mother's life and when he died, she poured all that love into Patrick."

"But…what about your father?"

"I never knew him. He was married, had another family. His *real* family," he said, blinking back stupid tears pricking his eyes. Looked like shoving feelings you didn't want to deal with down deep just buried them instead of eradicating them.

She gripped his hand tighter. "That's terrible. Your poor mother."

He exhaled a mirthless laugh. "Nah. No other man could hold a candle to the love of her life. She said my father was just some mistake she made."

"So you never knew him?"

"No. I think my mother agreed not to make trouble for his other family as long as he sent support checks. The checks arrived monthly like clockwork until I turned eighteen."

"You never wanted to meet him once you became an adult?"

He rubbed his chest but the constriction wouldn't ease up. "I found him and we spoke, but once my curiosity was satisfied I never felt the need for more."

But that was a lie, because he *had* felt the need. How could he desire a relationship with someone who'd shown no interest in him? "After Patrick died, my mother checked out. She was still physically there, going through the motions, but that was all. As a kid, I was afraid she'd kill herself and I'd be left with no one. As an adult, it made me angry and sad."

She shook her head. "She had you. That's terrible that she couldn't see that."

"My brother was a great guy, no question, but he wasn't perfect, nor was he a saint. But after his death, he'd become the anointed one who could do no wrong. I couldn't compete with a ghost."

"You shouldn't have had to. Is…is that why you don't like Christmas?"

Her voice was thick and when he touched her cheek, his fingers came away wet. The back of his throat burned. She was crying for him and he'd lied to her. "I lied."

"What?" She sniffled. "What did you lie about?"

"I lied when I said I never felt the need for a relationship with my father. I had hoped maybe he'd want a relationship, too. I had convinced myself he regretted his actions." He couldn't keep the bitterness from his tone. "I had this whole fairy-tale scenario built up in my head. Yeah, right."

She sucked in a sharp breath and laid her hand on his thigh. "You had every right to expect more than what you got from him. I'd love to give him a piece of my mind."

Her hand had curled into a fist and he laid his hand over the tight little ball. Such fierceness on his behalf. He uncurled her fingers as the tightness he'd carried in his chest for so long unfurled.

When she sniffed, he put his hands under her arms and dragged her on top of him and kissed her.

"No more tears," he whispered against her lips. "How can we take your mind off all this?"

"Well…" She stretched out on top of him. "I do have all these condoms. Can't let them go to waste."

He chuckled. "They do have expiration dates."

"Natalie?"

Someone was shaking her shoulder, trying to get her to wake up, but she wanted to cuddle up next to… an empty spot. Des wasn't next to her as he had been when she drifted off.

She opened one eye. "Des?"

"It's me." He kissed her forehead.

She opened both eyes and sat up.

Des was leaning over the bed, fully dressed. She glanced around and squinted at the glowing numbers of her alarm clock. It was half past midnight.

"I know you wanted me to leave before Sam got up."

Yeah, she'd said something to that effect before falling asleep. "I didn't mean to make it sound like I was kicking you out, but thank you for honoring my wishes."

"No problem. It's starting to snow so it's best to go now, but if we have an accumulation I'll be back to get you plowed out."

She yawned. "Doesn't the town plow?"

He chuckled. "I meant your driveway, unless you have a snowblower."

She swung her feet over the side of the bed. Standing, she reached for the robe on the bench across the end of the bed. Once she was covered up with pink terry cloth, she switched on the lamp. "No, but I did buy a snow shovel."

"If the forecast is right, we could get over a foot."

She tied the robe's belt. "I bought Sam a child-sized one, too."

"Well, in that case…"

She pushed his shoulder. "I told you, a little snow isn't going to scare me away."

"That's good." He hitched his chin toward the opened box of condoms on the bedside table. "We barely made a dent in your supply."

She patted his chest. "I have no complaints."

Yes, it had been a while—three years—since she'd been intimate with a man, but that didn't explain the incredible night with Des. Adding to their fantastic chemistry was the fact that he'd confided in her, trusted her with a piece of himself he didn't show anyone else. Now she understood him better and had hope for a future together. As trite as it might sound, the world, *her* world, looked bright and inviting.

His arms went around her and hers around him and their lips locked in a kiss that held a promise of more.

There was a noise at the door and he stepped away.

She went to the door, unlocked it and opened it a crack. The cat pranced in and gave her an accusing look and twitched his tail. She bent down and picked him up.

"I usually leave my door open a crack so he can come and go. He divides his time between me and Sam during the night," she explained to Des.

He scratched the cat's ears and tried to give her another kiss, but Shadow stuck his head in the way. "Good thing I'm in such a good mood."

Yeah, she was in a pretty sweet mood, too. A couple rounds of lovemaking would do that.

"If there's some accumulation in the morning, sit tight and I'll come over. You're not used to driving in this."

"But I need to help with the horses. Besides, I will need to learn to drive in the snow because I am here to stay."

"I'll take care of the horses in the morning. And let the plows clear the roads before you get out, promise?"

She scowled at him. "I'll have you know, Mr. Bossy Pants, I've been driving for ten years."

He quirked an eyebrow. "In the snow?"

She stuck her tongue out at him. "Brat."

His gaze zeroed in on her tongue, and his eyes darkened. He seemed to be fighting a battle with himself. Finally, he kissed her again and licked his lips when he ended the kiss. "Remember this. We won't be able to use up your king-size box if you're in traction."

"You do have a point," she conceded, already looking forward to their next encounter.

She followed Des to the door and gave him a kiss. "I want you to know I won't be asking you to make Christmas ornaments again."

He cocked his head to the side as his gaze met hers. "No?"

"It was unfair of me and I want you to know I respect your right not to want to make them. I shouldn't have pursued it once you said you didn't want to do it."

"Thanks, but I am glad you didn't give up easily." He touched the side of her face.

"Me, too, but I wanted you to know I regret pushing you." She leaned into his touch. "But know this. That's the one and only thing I regret."

"I'm glad," he whispered as his lips met hers in a kiss full of promise.

"Me, too."

"Until tomorrow," he said and opened the door.

Hugging the cat, she stood in the front window and watched Des get in his truck and back out of the driveway, missing his warmth already. Her thoughts drifted back to the days leading up to Ryan's death. They'd been arguing over her desire to finish her degree. Ryan had felt it was unnecessary, expensive and time consuming, but she'd disagreed. He'd wanted to talk about it, but she'd been too angry to discuss it rationally so she'd refused. Things had been tense and they'd had no time to apologize and make up before he died.

Anger had prevented her from telling him she loved him before he and Sam had left that day. She'd had every expectation he'd return home and they'd talk about it and come to a mutual decision. She stood for a long time, staring out the window, watching the snowflakes in the streetlight at the end of the road.

She'd fallen in love with Des Gallagher. This was no crush, no sex high. Well, okay, she might still be a little drunk on the passion they'd engaged in, but she was mature enough to separate the two. She'd fallen for him before tonight. How could she not fall for him after seeing how he treated Sam? Des had fit into their lives like a missing puzzle piece.

The cat was kneading its claws on her terry-cloth robe and purring in her ear.

Sighing, she went back down the hall toward her room, glancing into Sam's as she passed. The nightlight cast enough light so she could see he was still fast asleep. Setting the cat down, she went back to her room, put a nightgown on and crawled back into bed. Alone. For now. As she cuddled under the covers with Shadow curled up next to her, she pictured the future. Her and Des sharing a bed every night with no need for him to leave before Sam woke up.

Ryan's death had shown her how random and cruel life could be, but meeting Des had proved that some of life's most wonderful things could also be random.

Chapter Eight

Natalie awoke the next morning to the weight of an eight-pound cat sitting on her chest and a five-year-old boy poking her shoulder.

She lifted Shadow and sat up. "What is it?"

Sam ran to the window and lifted the blind and stuck his head between it and the glass.

"Did it snow?"

She grabbed her robe from the bench and threw it on. At the window she pulled up the blinds, and the cat jumped on the windowsill. Sam kept pointing to the snow. There were a few flurries coming down, but it appeared the major snowfall had stopped. She couldn't be sure.

"Yes, we'll go out, but first, breakfast." And coffee. She needed caffeine. "Go get dressed while I make breakfast."

She threw on a sweatshirt and jeans, stuck her feet into pink fuzzy slippers and went to the kitchen. She had to admit she was excited, too. And it had nothing to do with Des saying he'd come over to help with snow removal. Nothing? How about everything?

She considered the fact that he'd confided his feelings about his father as a big step forward in their relationship. Des wasn't someone who confided in people. That, combined with how he and Sam had bonded, gave her hopes for them as a family. Maybe even more children in the future.

After putting a pod in the coffeemaker, she got out eggs and bread. She'd be lucky if she could get Sam to eat more than a few bites but scrambled eggs and toast would be quick to make.

She was beating the eggs when a horn tooted. Des? She set the bowl down and moved the frying pan off the burner. There was a knock at the front door before she could reach it. Sam came galloping down the hall with one sock on and the other in his hand, the cat nipping at his heels.

"Sam," she cautioned, but he was already opening the door.

Des filled the doorway and she fumbled a bit trying to get the storm door unlocked. She managed to push the little knob and opened the door.

"Hey, guys." Des stepped inside bringing the cold, crisp winter air with him. It seemed to cling to him along with a faint woodsmoke scent.

Sam pointed outside while Des stamped the snow off his boots before stepping into the house and shutting the door.

Des ruffled Sam's hair. "Yeah. Lots of snow out there, bud, but I think you need something more on your feet first."

"And he needs to eat some breakfast," she said. "Maybe Des will join us for some eggs and toast."

"If your mom's cooking, you better believe I'm eating." Des unzipped his jacket and hung it on the coat rack next to the door, then removed his boots. He set them on the plastic tray next to a pair of Natalie's shoes.

"Sam, put your other sock on." She turned her attention to Des. "You're early. Did you take care of the horses already?"

"Sure did." He touched her arm and smiled.

"Have you had breakfast yet?"

He made a face. "Does a Pop-Tart count?"

Both socks on, Sam stood up and gave Des a thumbs-up.

"A Pop-Tart does not count. We're having eggs and toast."

Sam pointed to her and shook his head.

Des laughed. "I think Sam is saying you're…absolutely right. Eggs and toast is a much healthier breakfast."

Sam put his hands on his hips and gave Des a scowl.

"You're gonna get me in trouble with your mom," Des told him and pretended to shadow box.

Sam burst out laughing and pushed Des toward the kitchen.

"Eggs it is," he said, and when Sam's head was turned, he gave her a quick peck on the cheek.

In the kitchen, she broke more eggs into the bowl and switched to a bigger frying pan. Watching Sam and

Des together these past weeks had given her mixed feelings. She was happy they got along so well together, but knew it was already too late to prevent Sam from getting hurt if things didn't work out with her and Des. She glanced at Des. Yeah, Sam wouldn't be the only one getting hurt. She fell in love with Des a little more each time she was with him.

Sam took a seat at the table and began to draw with crayons and a pad that were on the table.

"How can I help?" Des asked.

Fall in love with me, too. "If you want coffee, there are some pods next to the maker. Mugs are in the cabinet above it. Help yourself." She motioned to the coffeemaker.

He picked out a pod and took a mug from the cupboard. "Do you want some?"

"I haven't finished the first yet." She indicated her mug next to the stove. "Although I may need another shot of caffeine to get going."

"Someone tire you out last night?" He gave her a bland expression but his eyes darkened.

Despite the fluttering in her chest, she returned his bland expression. Not an easy feat when she wanted to giggle like a schoolgirl or break into song as if she were Julie Andrews on an Austrian mountain meadow. "Something like that."

Sam got up and handed Des a picture he'd drawn.

Des held up the picture. "I think he wants to build a snowman. Right, bud?"

Sam nodded and Des playfully poked him and made him giggle.

"And so we shall. As soon as we eat our eggs and toast," Des said.

Natalie mouthed "thank you" to Des and dished out the eggs onto a platter and put buttered toast on a plate. She brought them to the table. All they were doing was eating breakfast together but she felt a thrill run through her each time her gaze landed on Des. What would it be like to have this scenario be her future? Waking up to Des every morning, and better yet, going to bed each night with him. Sharing their lives and love. *Don't go getting ahead of yourself, Natalie.*

As soon as Sam had shoveled in the last bite, he jumped up and went to get his jacket and new snow boots. He shoved his feet into the boots and Natalie showed him how the pull-tie laces worked. She gathered her dirty dishes and piled them in the sink.

"Want help with that?" Des gathered the rest of the plates.

She shook her head. "I'll worry about them later. Sam wants to get out there before it all melts."

Des laughed. "No chance of that. It's still coming down."

She shrugged. "Like I said, if we got any snow in Nashville, it disappeared as soon as the sun came out."

"Not much chance of that here."

She grinned and motioned with her head toward the front door. Sam was bouncing up and down, waiting to go out. Des met her gaze and grinned in silent communication.

After getting her parka buttoned up, she put on a knit cap and mittens.

Des glanced at her feet. "Did you get new boots, too?"

"I took your warnings to heart." She put her palm flat on his chest. "I've been taking notes and learning. So be warned, you're not getting rid of me that easily."

He put his hands on each side of her waist. "What makes you think I'm trying to get rid of you?"

"You keep warning me about the snow."

He squeezed his hands around her waist. "I'm looking out for you. Not chasing you away."

She exhaled in relief. "I'm glad because I like it here in Loon Lake and I like you."

"I—"

Sam tugged on Des's sleeve and pointed outside. Des released her and put his hand over Sam's head, adjusting his knit cap. "Okay, bud, let's go build the best snowman Loon Lake has ever seen."

Natalie's heart clenched. What had Des been about to say? Had he been going to return the sentiment? Or could he have been about to warn her not to take this seriously? Tell her not to read too much into what they'd shared last night?

"You guys go out. I want to get some things for the snowman's face." *And to collect myself.* Let feelings that were too close to the surface settle back down. Des had been the first man she'd become sexually intimate with since the death of her husband, so naturally her feelings would be confusing.

She got a carrot and coffee beans from the kitchen and found an old scarf and mittens in a box of things she'd been collecting to donate. Taking a breath and telling herself not to read too much into a comment that Des never even finished, she ventured outside.

"First, we need to make the body parts. Do you know how to do that, Sam?"

Sam shrugged and Des patted his shoulder. "Don't worry, it's easy."

Natalie noticed Des had picked up her habit of asking Sam specific questions, ones that he could answer with a yes or no movement of his head. She often wondered if she should be doing more to encourage Sam to use his tablet for communication. Or was letting him develop at his own pace the answer? Since being with Des, Sam seemed more willing to use his tablet. Maybe Sam's therapist's cautious optimism was warranted.

Des demonstrated how to roll out parts for a snowman with Sam helping him. The two of them pushed the large balls of snow around the yard. Des glanced up at her when they'd gotten the requisite three balls stacked up. She handed him the carrot she'd gotten out of the vegetable bin for a nose, some fresh coffee beans for a smile plus an old scarf and knitted cap to complete his outfit.

"Do you have any old pants or boots Sam maybe had outgrown?"

"As a matter of fact, I have a box of stuff I hadn't gotten around to taking to the charity shop. What did you have in mind?"

"You'll see."

She ran in the house and got the box. Des was whispering something to Sam when she got back. They'd put another small ball on top of the snowman.

Sam ran to the box with a huge grin on his face and pulled out pants and an old pair of boots.

"What have you two cooked up?"

"You'll see," Des said and took the things from Sam. "Thanks, bud. We'll use the leftovers for another face." He glanced at Sam. "Okay?"

Sam retrieved the things from the porch and held out his hand to Des, who shook his head. "I'll hold you up and you do it. Do you want to do that?"

Sam's eyes widened and he nodded. Des held up the smaller ball of snow on top of the snowman's head. He held him in place while Sam placed the items to make another face.

"A two-headed snowman?" Natalie asked.

Des and Sam shook their heads at the same time and Natalie's heart expanded until she thought it would burst. Was she doing the right thing letting Sam get this close to Des when there was no guarantee things would work out between the adults? If they didn't, Sam could be collateral damage. But then, sacrificing her personal life might not be the right answer for her child. If she was unhappy or lonely, she wouldn't be setting a good example for Sam.

Des set Sam back on the ground and headed for his truck. "I think I have some rope. Sam, get some old shirts or something from that box so we can fill out the pants so they look like legs."

Des and Sam stuffed an old pair of pajamas into the pants and Des pushed the rope through and tied the old boots to each end before placing them on the snowman.

Natalie stood back and watched. "Oh, my, look at that. Let me find extra mittens and a knit hat."

In the garage she found some extra mittens and a hat and gave them to Des. He finished arranging the snowman and once they got it finished, it looked like an adult snowman carrying a snow child on his shoulders.

Sam kept grinning and pointing to the snowman. She nodded and gave him a thumbs up. Despite all her optimistic thoughts this morning, her stomach quivered. After one night with Des, she couldn't let her desire go rampaging ahead because Sam needed to be considered in every decision she made.

"Your first snowman and it's a masterpiece." Natalie hugged Sam. "Teddy will be so surprised when he and Miss Addie get back."

"Where's your neighbor?" Des asked.

"They went to visit friends in Massachusetts for the weekend." She studied their snow masterpiece and felt proud. Sam was beside himself with excitement. No matter what the future held, today would be a treasured memory. One they could look back on with joy.

She patted the snowman. "What made you think of this?"

"I'm an artist... I'm supposed to be creative. It's part of the job description." His cheeks had color in them. Whether from the cold air or embarrassment, she couldn't tell.

"You're right. Sorry. I should've realized."

He gave a sharp bark of laughter. "I saw it on Pinterest."

"You use Pinterest?"

He shrugged. "It makes it easier to keep track of some of my designs and inspiration for future works."

"I see," she said. She suspected he wore that gruffness like an outer shell to protect his soft underbelly. She treasured those glimpses beneath his surly exterior.

He grunted. "You see what?"

"You." She smiled. "I see you, Des Gallagher."

"Of course you do." He gave her a quizzical look. "I'm standing right in front of you. Let me get the snowblower from the back of the truck and I'll get your sidewalks cleared."

"Let me get my new shovel and I'll clear off the front steps. The logistics of snow removal are still new to me."

Sam nodded his head and tugged on Natalie's sleeve and pointed to the plow attached to the truck.

"He wants to know if you're going to use the plow."

Des laughed. "It might be a bit of overkill, but if he wants to hop in the back, we can clear your driveway and your neighbor's."

She nodded. "Thanks. As the landlord, I am responsible."

He turned to Sam. "You want to ride in the truck with me while we plow?"

Sam grabbed Des's hand and nodded.

"Okay, but you have to ride in the back, bud."

"I'll have to get his booster seat out of my car."

"I already have one back there."

"You do?" Natalie was surprised and pleased he had gone to the trouble of getting one for Sam. What did the gesture mean? Or did he think it would make things easier when they went around collecting items for the auction?

"Yeah. I remembered what kind you had and picked one up last time I was in town."

She swallowed. "Thanks."

He opened the rear door on the driver's side and gave Sam a boost. "You want to check and make sure I did it right?"

She made sure Sam was buckled in securely, not an easy task considering he was bouncing with excitement. "I hate to ask but could you plow the lady across the street's driveway, too?" She pointed to the Cape Cod–style home across the street. "Mrs. O'Malley's in her eighties and a widow."

While Des worked, she went and got her brand-new snow shovel from the carport and cleared off the front steps on both sides of the duplex.

After plowing, Des got the snowblower from where he had it secured in the back of the truck and did the sidewalks, including Mrs. O'Malley's. Sam used his shovel to clear off the widow's steps while Des did the sidewalk. Natalie stood on her own steps and watched the two of them working. *Her two men.* What? No, she needed to not read too much into this with Des.

The elderly woman came to the door, and Sam and Des stood talking to her. She handed something to Sam and went back inside. "What you got there, Sam?" she asked as the two came back across the street.

Sam held up a toy truck.

"She wanted to pay us but we said no," Des said. "But she insisted Sam needed the truck for his collection."

"She's so sweet. Did you thank her?" When Sam nodded, she continued, "How about we go inside and warm up with some hot chocolate? Sam?"

Natalie couldn't help notice that Sam looked to Des before nodding. Her stomach clenched when she realized all the implications of that simple gesture. Sure, she enjoyed the smile of happiness on Sam's face, but knowing Des put it there was troubling because she didn't know how long he'd be in their lives. Could she count on Des to be here after the auction? How would Sam feel if Des was out of their lives? She definitely needed to look into a Big Brother organization in or near Loon Lake.

They trooped back into the house through the carport. She helped Sam get out of his boots and jacket in the laundry room. "Go get some dry clothes on and bring me your wet pants."

Des leaned against the door frame as she set the wet socks, hat and mittens on the washing machine to deal with later.

"I think we'll—uh…" He cleared his throat. "I mean you'll need to get him snow pants to go over his jeans and the top of his boots if he's going to do a lot of playing in the snow this winter."

"Yeah, I guess I hadn't thought about him being in snow that deep. Shows how totally unprepared I am. The hand-knitted mittens were warm but not waterproof."

He stepped closer, put his arm around her and pressed his lips to her temple. "Like you said, it's your first winter here."

"Then it's a good thing I have someone like you to show me the ropes." She leaned into him, enjoying his solid strength. "Thank you for today."

Having Des to lean on thrilled and scared her. The future held no guarantees. Could she survive another devastating loss? But, by the same token, she couldn't let fear rule her decisions or rob her of a future with a wonderful—if sometimes grumpy—man.

Chapter Nine

Three days had passed since the season's first snow-fall and since the temperatures stayed below freezing, the white blanketing her yard, including Sam's snow-man, stuck around.

Natalie snuggled against Des as they enjoyed a few stolen hours together in her bed. Brody and Mary had included Sam in a group of kids they'd taken sledding and he'd been excited to go. They'd invited her to go along, but she'd felt it important to release, or at least relax, her grip on Sam's hand. She hoped there'd be many more outings like this in his future, and not just because it gave her and Des alone time they were putting to good use. And making a dent in her jumbo box of condoms.

She caressed her fingers across his chest. "Did you always want to be a pilot?"

"I was always interested in flying." He rubbed his hand up and down her arm.

"After your injuries couldn't you have been an instructor or something? Use your love of flying to teach the new guys." She hated the thought that he had to walk away from something he loved.

He yawned. "I might have been able to do something in the classroom."

"But you chose to walk away."

"I'm not saying I didn't love every minute of it—you have to love it in order to make it through the intense training—but…"

"What? Tell me?" She yearned to know everything she could about the man she'd fallen in love with.

"Flying had been Patrick's dream. After he died I guess I took it on as my own. Not consciously. I don't know… Maybe I thought my mother would transfer all those feelings she had for my brother to me."

"I'm guessing she didn't."

"No. Even in death Patrick always came first." He sighed. "I had always thought being the favorite was a good thing. I was even jealous of Patrick even though he was never anything but generous and protective with me."

"Do you know why he killed himself?"

"I can't be sure but I think having to live up to my mother's expectations added a lot of pressure on him."

"I'm sorry you were exposed to that much dysfunction."

"I survived."

"But it skewed your opinion of families."

He raised an eyebrow. "Has it? Or maybe you're the one with the skewed vision of families."

"I'd hate to think that." She shook her head. Suspecting he was jaded was one thing, but having him verify it another.

He gave her a pitying look. "That's because you're an eternal optimist, ignoring reality."

"Hey, that's not fair." He'd gotten her hackles up with his comments. That expression on his face hadn't helped. She didn't appreciate having to defend something like optimism. "Because I believe in happily-ever-after and happy families doesn't mean I live in a fantasy world."

"It does if they don't exist. Was your marriage to Sam's father perfect?"

Her hands curled into fists. "Of course not. I never said anything about perfection. It's not the same thing. A relationship doesn't have to be perfect to be happy or successful."

His words brought her guilt over the final days of her life with Ryan to the surface.

"Relationships aren't perfect or guaranteed, but we need to try." And she believed that.

"Why put yourself out there to get your heart broken?"

"Because if you don't, how can you say you lived? The people who never get their hearts broken are dead. Frankly, I don't aspire to be dead." The blood pounding in her ears made it difficult to focus on her thoughts. Why had she pursued this conversation when he was going to say things she didn't want to hear? Because burying her head in the sand wasn't the answer, either.

He made an impatient noise. "And you think I do?"

"Not consciously, but not feeling anything isn't living." Her heart broke for him. What an awful way to live.

"Opening your heart to someone, making yourself vulnerable, is asking for trouble. How can you sign up for that? You can't believe all that 'better to have loved and lost than not at all.'" He shook his head and looked at her as if he felt sorry for *her*.

She tried to swallow past the growing lump in her throat. She'd known Des was cynical, but she hadn't realized the extent and that knowledge made her stomach queasy. "I may have lost Ryan but I have Sam and I wouldn't trade any of the pain for not ever having known or loved him."

"Ah, jeez, Natalie, forgive me. I shouldn't have dumped all that on you." He urged her closer. "The last thing I want is to fight with you."

She didn't want to spend precious time with him fighting, either, but she wasn't sure she could accept his view of relationships. She could walk away from what they had, but what would that prove? Would it reinforce his beliefs? But if she stayed, she could show him that loving someone didn't have to lead to heartbreak. She owed it to both of them to try, except she couldn't hold up a relationship on her own. She knew he cared. He might not want to admit it, but his actions had proved that. Even if he denied it, he'd gone out of his way to show them how much he cared. All the things he'd done for and with her and Sam proved that. She might regret it for the rest of her life if she left now.

She relaxed and wrapped her arm around his waist.

Resting her head on his chest, she listened to his beating heart under her ear. "Me, too."

He put his hand under her chin, lifted her face to his and kissed her. "How much time do we have before Sam gets home?"

She smiled. "Enough time enough to make me glad I went with the jumbo box."

Des came back into the barn with the empty wheelbarrow and stood for a moment. Natalie was busy cleaning Augie's stall and he watched her. How had he become so involved with a woman who believed in the sitcom version of happy families? He'd opened up to someone who believed in fairy tales.

He blew out his breath and tried to ignore that uneasy feeling in the pit of his stomach.

"What time are you supposed to get Sam?" he asked as he brought the wheelbarrow to the stall.

She stopped raking shavings and turned toward him. "Addie will bring him home later this evening. Why?"

"I bumped into Brody Wilson the other day and he asked if we'd be interested in a sleigh ride out at his farm. He bought an old one and restored it as a Christmas gift for Mary. She's always wanted to go on a sleigh ride."

She laughed. "Leave it to Brody to buy a sleigh instead of just taking her on a ride."

"Yeah, the guy is a bit smitten. Anyway, he said we were welcome to come out and give the sleigh a try. I guess Riley and Meg Cooper have been out there. So I thought maybe you and I could check it out, just the two of us. Brody said to let him know." He set the wheelbarrow down. "That is, if you're interested."

"I'd love it. Thank you. I've never been on one." She beamed with pleasure. "My first winter in Loon Lake and I'm going on a sleigh ride."

Her reaction made him glad he'd asked her. From the moment he had run into Brody and learned about the sleigh rides, Des had wanted to take Natalie on one. He'd never been romantic, but this was something he wanted to do for her. As much as he enjoyed doing things with Sam along, he wanted to do this with and for Natalie. He was glad she'd felt the same.

He was still trying the ignore the queasiness whenever he remembered how much he'd revealed to this woman.

Had this thing between them moved to the next level too quickly? He knew nothing about maintaining a relationship. Maybe he should stick to the horses. Those he knew about, but the care and feeding of a relationship was beyond his experience.

He might know how to land a jet on a carrier in the middle of the ocean, but keeping a woman like Natalie happy long term…not so much. What did he have to give her?

How about starting with a sleigh ride, his inner voice suggested.

Once at the Wilson's farm, they found one of Brody's horses hitched to a two-person red-and-gold sled in front of the barn.

Des glanced around. "Looks like Brody has everything ready to go for us."

"This is wonderful. It's a one-horse open sleigh like in the song." She turned to him. "I love it."

Her breathless voice tightened his groin and he urged her close for a kiss.

"Ahem."

Caught. Des stepped away but his lips twitched at Natalie's amused grin despite the color staining her cheeks.

"Glad you two could make it," Brody said as he strolled out of the open double doors of the barn.

Natalie threw her arms around Brody in a friendly hug. "Thank you so much for the opportunity. I've never been on a sleigh ride and I've been looking forward to this one ever since Des mentioned it."

"You're most welcome. I hope you feel the same way after the ride." Brody laughed and kissed Natalie's cheek. "I'm glad Scrooge here brought you."

Des scowled at Brody, who had the nerve to laugh.

"In case you get cold." Brody pointed to a plaid wool blanket folded up on the seat.

She nodded. "I make sure to dress in layers wherever I go these days."

Des put his arm around her shoulder. "We'll make a Vermonter out of you yet."

"Says the man who's only been here three years longer than me." She playfully pushed him.

"I hate to break it to you two, but you're both 'flatlanders,' as Tavie would say." Brody laughed.

"So are you," Des told him.

"Yeah, well, we can't all be perfect," Brody said.

Natalie, who was preparing to get in the sleigh, turned around. "Guys, what's a flatlander?"

"It's what the native Vermonters call someone who wasn't born here." Des put his hand under her elbow. "Let me help you up."

After helping her, Des swung up onto the sleigh and settled on the seat beside her. He arranged the blanket around them.

Brody patted the horse. "Ranger knows what to do and he knows his way home. Have fun, you two."

Des clucked to the horse, who took off with a jingle of bells.

"This is perfect." Natalie sighed and cuddled against him.

Des put his arm around her and drew her closer, kissing her temple. This was everything he had imagined. He hadn't done it for any other reason than to be with her and bask in the glow from her smile. He ignored the warning voice that suggested he might be getting in too deep with Natalie. She wasn't looking for anything more than what they had because she had a son to raise, he argued with himself.

He put one arm around her as he held the reins loosely in his other hand. Brody had been right. The horse knew the trail and kept to it at a moderate pace with little guidance from him. Good thing, because his thoughts were with the woman beside him. Maybe he'd come out and ask her what she was expecting from what they were sharing. She snuggled closer and sighed. Maybe now wasn't the best time for that sort of a discussion.

"Des, look," Natalie whispered and touched his arm.

A doe and her fawn were visible through the woods. He halted the horse so they could watch the small family until they wandered back off into the woods.

The deer disappeared from view, but Des kept his gaze on the spot where they'd been nibbling on the bushes. Could he keep Natalie and Sam from disappearing from his life as the deer had so easily moved on?

"It's perfect. Thank you," she said after the deer had wandered back into the woods. "Huh, seems like I'm always thanking you for something. But you've made this Christmas memorable. Not bad for a guy who tries to make everyone think he's Scrooge."

He shook his head. "You've ruined my reputation."

She laughed. "Sorry?"

The horse tugged at the reins, so Des loosened his grip. "I think he's wanting to get back to home."

"I guess I can't blame him. It's getting late but we did have a wonderful ride."

"I'm glad you enjoyed it," he told her and kissed her, putting his worries about what the future might hold on the back burner for now.

The horse sped up as if in a hurry to get back home and Natalie snuggled closer to Des, wringing the last bit of enjoyment out of their adventure.

Back at the barn, Brody came out and took charge of Ranger. Des jumped down and turned to help her. He offered to assist Brody with the horse and sled, but Brody waved him off.

After thanking Brody and asking after Mary and Elliott who, according to Brody, were out Christmas shopping, they shook his hand and got in Des's pickup.

As Des was driving down the long gravel driveway, Natalie got a text from Addie asking if Sam could go with her and Teddy to the movies.

Natalie told Des, adding, "That means we have a couple more hours to ourselves. Will you come to my place?"

"Sure." He arched his eyebrows. "Any suggestions for using those hours?"

"I could make cocoa and we could watch a movie. Or…" She couldn't hide her grin. "I do have that somewhat large supply of condoms…"

"I like the way you think." Des took her hand and intertwined his fingers with hers for the rest of the drive back to her place.

"Did you want anything to drink…or anything?" she asked as they walked up the sidewalk and went inside her house.

Inside, she removed her coat and hung it on a hook attached to the wall in the entryway, suddenly feeling nervous.

They'd joked about using up her condom supply, but having a casual sexual relationship was new territory for her. Were there certain protocols? She—

"Hey, where'd you go?" he asked and placed his hands over hers to still her hand wringing.

She glanced down at their hands. How could she put into words what she was feeling?

He put a finger under her chin and lifted her face to his. His dark gaze searched her face. "If you've changed your mind…"

She swallowed. "I haven't."

He tucked her hair behind her ear and traced the outer edge of her ear with his finger. "You sure?"

"I'm positive." She huffed out a nervous laugh. "I'm

sure you're thinking I'm the silliest woman you've ever met, but I'm just…this is all new to me."

"You're not silly." He rubbed a knuckle down her cheek. "You're the most special woman I've ever known and I'm so glad I met you."

She turned her head and kissed his hand. "I think you mean you're glad I barged into your life and refused to go away."

"No matter how much I growled at you." He caressed her bottom lip. "And I'm thankful you didn't turn tail and run."

"You're saying that because you know you're about to get lucky."

He shook his head. "I've been lucky since you walked into my barn and I'm not referring to what's hopefully about to happen."

She took his hand and they walked to her bedroom.

Afterward she cuddled up next to him and heaved a contented sigh. "This is one of the many reasons why I fell in love with you."

His body tensed and the sudden change in him confused her. A wave of nausea hit her when she realized what she'd said. She hadn't meant to make the big confession now, but the words had slipped out. She might not have meant to say it yet, but she wasn't going to take it back. Her feelings were too big to hold in any longer and she felt giddy with relief at it being out in the open. Trying to hold it in had begun to feel as if she were hiding something, and she hated lying. The truth was she loved him. Plain and simple. She might not be able to pinpoint when it happened or how, but there was no turning back. She was lost.

He pulled away and sat up. "I wish you hadn't said that."

She recoiled as his words pelted her like hail. "Why? Why shouldn't I say it? It's true. It's been true for a while now."

He rubbed his hand over his face. "I thought we were going to keep this casual."

Casual? She might not have had a lot of sexual experience, but even she knew what was between them was special. And yes, she knew sexual chemistry wasn't the same as love, but they'd shared a lot more than what had happened between the sheets. Her throat closed and swallowing became painful. The future that had been so clear hours ago began to dissolve into nothingness. But she only had herself to blame, because all those fantasies of their future together were just that— stories she'd made up in her head. She'd been falling head over heels in love and he'd been doing casual. "When did we say that? Was there a book of rules I should have been following?"

"See? This is what happens when that word is thrown around." His tone and his expression grew hard and resentful.

She flinched at his reply, suggesting he was blaming her for falling in love with *him*. Maybe if he hadn't been so irresistible she wouldn't have fallen in love. So it was his fault. What was wrong with her? You couldn't assign blame when falling in love. It just happened. "That word? You mean *love*?"

"Yeah, that's the one." He jumped out of bed and punctuated the statement by pointing his index finger at her. Anger hardened his features.

"You can't even say it." How could she have gotten this so wrong? Her face grew hot with humiliation. She'd told him she loved him and he was treating her as if she'd done something wrong. As if her *love* was wrong.

"What's happened? What has changed? We're both still the same people we were before I said those words," she said, hating the pleading note in her voice.

But she knew that wasn't true. She had changed it by saying those words. Words he didn't want, wasn't ready to hear because he couldn't even say *love*, let alone mean it. Maybe this was all her fault. No! The only thing she'd done wrong was to fall for a man with so much baggage that he couldn't even say the word. He might never be in a place to be able to process the love she and Sam were offering him. She couldn't think like that. She wasn't going to think like that.

He began pulling on his pants. "I thought we were on the same page but obviously I was wrong."

"Obviously," she repeated drily. She sighed and rolled off the bed and grabbed her robe from the bench at the end of the bed. She needed to cover up, as if pink terry cloth could shield her from all the pain barreling through her system. She pulled the robe tight around her, trying to contain the pain; otherwise her heart would shatter and the pieces would scatter like confetti. She'd never get them all back.

"I'm sorry you find my being in love with you so offensive." Her voice was hoarse and barely recognizable.

He blew his breath out noisily and shoved his arms into his flannel shirt. "I never said anything like that. You're putting words in my mouth. I just—"

Her sorrow turned into frustration and anger. "Maybe you didn't say exactly those things, but as soon as I said I love you, you began searching for your clothes. Now you're halfway out the door. Your about-face has given me whiplash."

"Natalie, I—"

"No. Don't you dare." She spat the words at him. "I'm not going to apologize for loving you, Des Gallagher."

He made a derisive snort and slashed the air with his hand. "You may not apologize, but you'll regret it. Maybe not today. Maybe not even tomorrow. But someday. My own mother couldn't love me… Ashley didn't… How can you?"

"I don't know what your mother's problem was…but the problem was with her. Not you. If she didn't love you or treated you less than you deserved, it's on her. Not you." She hadn't felt this helpless since the day a drunk driver plowed into a crowd of innocent people, changing her life. "As for Ashley… I'm not even going to say what I think of her."

"I never asked you into my life. You barged in and kept coming back despite the things I said. Or have you conveniently forgotten that?"

"No, but it sounds as if you've forgotten what you said an hour ago."

He scowled. "What? What did I say?"

"Nothing of any importance." But it had been important. His words had made her feel as special as he'd said, maybe had even given her the courage to confess how she felt. Those words had changed her life and he couldn't remember them. She swayed and had to lock her knees to remain standing. Putting her hand on the bedside chair for support, she asked, "Let me get this straight so there's no mistake. You're saying you don't want me in your life?"

"Maybe I don't want to be another one of your damned projects! Maybe I liked my life just fine before you came barging in with your endless chatter and fattening cookies."

Natalie closed her eyes as she tried to manage the agony shooting through her body. Ryan's death had hurt and she'd mourned him, but somehow this was much worse. Des was intentionally hurting her, causing the pain on purpose. Inserting the knife and rotating it until all her tender organs bled.

"Natalie, I shouldn't have said any of that. It was mean and nasty, meant to hurt. I'm so sorry. I—"

"No, don't." She held up her hand. Ice spread through her belly. "I'm the one who wanted honesty, remember? Huh, what is that saying? 'Be careful what you wish for.'"

"I shouldn't have said any of that. Please believe me." Now his tone was pleading, as if he was asking her to forgive him.

Unable to take on his pain, too, she didn't know if she had enough strength to handle her own right now. And Sam. Oh, my God, what would this do to him? She should have protected Sam, stepped in when she saw they were bonding.

She shook her head. "If that's how you feel, then you should speak your mind. I'm an adult. I won't lie and say it didn't hurt, but it's better to know how you feel. What I can't forgive you for is Sam. Have you shown any consideration for him?"

He looked flummoxed. "I have been nothing but kind to him."

His expression would've been comical if this whole situation wasn't so damn tragic. "You made him love you. Now you want to back off. He's five... How is he supposed to process that when I, as an adult, can't?"

"What I said... I shouldn't have. I was angry." He reached out his hand, but dropped it when she flinched.

"Does...does my loving you make you angry? Because I never wanted that. And if I could stop loving you, I would. You're not an easy man to love, Des Gallagher. And right now it doesn't feel very good. But that's not how this whole falling-in-love thing works. I couldn't stop it and I can't turn it off so maybe...maybe you should go."

She needed him to leave. Anguish was threatening to overcome her rigid control. If she lost control, she'd be a blubbering mess, saying things she'd regret. Like begging him for things he couldn't or wouldn't give. Des had the upper hand because she'd admitted she loved him, but she still had her pride. Pride might be all she had and it was cold comfort, but it was hers and she was hanging on to it.

"I hate leaving having you think I meant those things." He reached out again, but she backed away. "Natalie, please."

"What you did or did not mean isn't the issue. Clearly my saying I love you freaked you out to the point you lashed out." Her eyes burned but she held back the tears by opening her eyes as wide as she could. She'd cry later when she was alone, because it wasn't going to be pretty.

"I don't see why we couldn't go along the way we were," he muttered.

"Because I have a son and every relationship, every bond, I form with anyone involves and impacts him. He's a little boy and my first duty is to him. I can't have men come and go from his life as if it doesn't matter."

"Christ. I'm not about to abandon him." He rubbed his scalp. "I'm talking about messy emotions between you and I."

"But I can't turn my messy emotions off. I feel what I feel and I'm not sure suppressing them is healthy and now, what I said is hanging out there. I can't take it back…and maybe I don't want to take it back. Maybe ending this is best for all of us. I have an impressionable son to think about. I want him to grow up respecting women and—"

He stiffened as if she'd struck him. "Are you saying I don't respect you?"

"No, but I want Sam to grow up understanding that in a healthy relationship both parties share their feelings. That—" she swallowed "—one party isn't carrying the whole burden."

"What will you tell him about…about us?"

"The truth," she managed through frozen lips. "I'll tell him that sometimes adults can't make relationships work and they end up hurting one another so it's best to go their separate ways."

"Natalie…"

"I think we've said all that needs to be said. I'd like you to go."

When he reached the door, he stopped with his hand

on the knob and turned back, his gaze meeting hers in a silent plea. She closed her eyes.

The door opened, then shut with a soft click that reverberated through her entire body like a sonic boom.

Chapter Ten

Des finished cleaning Augie's stall and moved like a robot onto the next one. It had been two days since the scene in Natalie's bedroom. Each hour that passed had him feeling sicker and sicker. He hadn't been able to sleep for more than an hour at a time and his stomach had refused all but coffee and antacid tablets.

The upside was that his bum leg was the least of his problems and the horse stalls were spotless because the physical labor suited him. Too bad he wasn't a drinking man. He might have been able to find some oblivion, but he was afraid if he did, he wouldn't be able to find his way back. Another legacy from his mother: addiction.

You made him love you.

Natalie's accusing words echoed and pierced him like those shards of broken glass he used for his sculptures.

He wore gloves to protect his hands while handling the sharp pieces. Too bad he couldn't have protected his heart just as easily.

How many times had he walked to his truck to go to Natalie's, only to turn around and come back to the barn? What had she told Sam? What was there to say?

Pulling the roll from his pocket, he popped another antacid into his mouth and chewed. His own father had one up on him, because he'd never formed a relationship with his child. Instead, Des himself was guilty of forming a bond with a little boy, then disappearing.

Natalie was there to soothe Sam's broken heart, but who would be there for *her*? Was she baking cookies? Was the cat still chasing the train? Was Sam using his iPad to communicate more? All questions he had no answers to and might never get. What had he done? He'd blown the best thing that had ever happened to him. He blinked trying to clear his vision, but the blurring remained.

He wiped his eyes on his sleeve before tackling another stall when the sound of a truck pulling up stopped him. Setting aside the rake, he left the barn.

Des saw the horse trailer and his stomach turned to stone. This couldn't be good. *You got that right, Gallagher.* Nothing had been good since that night Natalie ruined what they had going on. A voice shouted that the fault was his and his alone, and as much as he tried he couldn't drown it out. His biggest mistake had been trying to be someone he wasn't. Take that stupid sleigh ride for example. He never should've suggested it. He wasn't a romantic guy.

He shaded his eyes from the sun using his hand. "Brody, what are you doing here?"

"Gallagher?" Brody peered at him. "Hey, man, you look like crap."

"Is that what you came all the way out here to tell me?" He rubbed his forehead, hoping to ease the headache he'd had for two days.

"Nah. I suspect you feel as bad as you look." Brody gave him a pitying look. "Natalie asked me to come and get the horses."

His one link to sanity and she wanted to take that away. Des leaned on the rake. "Does she have a place to board them?"

Brody blew out his breath. "I barely have room but I agreed to take Augie for the time being. The rest are being boarded about thirty miles away until a decision is made about the future of the program."

Thirty miles? Natalie must hate him if she'd let those horses go so far away. "Let me help you get them loaded up."

"Thanks." Brody gave him a calculating glance. "Sounds like you messed up."

Des stiffened at the thought of someone knowing his personal business. What did it matter? Anyone looking at him could tell what a mess he was and pretty much everyone in town would know why. He had been all around town with Natalie and Sam acting as if they were a family. As if he believed in happy families. As if someone like him could be a part of one.

"I'll take that brooding look as a yes." Brody laughed and shook his head. "You remind me of how I was when I nearly blew it with Mary."

"You did?" He didn't know Brody well but he knew from seeing him and Mary together and from town gossip that the Wilsons had a solid relationship.

Brody grimaced as if the memory was painful. "I had to watch her walk out of my life to catch on and smarten up."

"But you're so happy together now."

"Yeah, had to swallow my pride and admit I'd messed up." Brody clapped him on the shoulder. "But it was worth it."

Des shook his head. "You may have worked things out, but I'm not that guy. I'm not like you and Riley."

"What a load of horse manure." Brody laughed again. "Hey, man, we all put our pants on a leg at a time."

Des rolled his eyes. "Let me help you get these horses loaded."

Brody threw up his hands. "So you're giving up? Just like that?"

"You don't understand." Des crossed his arms over his chest.

Brody snorted a laugh. "Yeah, that's what I told Riley Cooper when he tried to talk some sense into me."

It was too late for that. Someone should've talked some sense into him before he'd spoken those awful words. "I'm sure my situation is a lot worse than yours. I said some unforgivable things."

"But see, you don't get to decide that." Brody pulled a toothpick from his shirt pocket, unwrapped it and shoved it into his mouth.

"What do you mean?" He swiped his sweaty palms down his pants.

"Natalie is the only one who can decide if what you

said or did was unforgivable. She's the one that will have to do the forgiving, so it's all up to her." Brody rolled the toothpick around in his mouth before taking it out. "Mary forgave me for being a jackass and from what Riley has told me, Meg did the same for him. Seems women have a great capacity for forgiveness. I'm not saying they won't call us out when we're wrong, 'cause they will, but they also forgive us because they know we can't help messing up."

Was it possible that he hadn't messed up his chances with Natalie? Did he want another chance to be with her and Sam? More than he wanted to fly again, more than he'd wanted anything else in his entire life. He might have suppressed it, but he'd ached to be part of a family, a happy, normal family, all his life. That's why he'd ignored the warning signs in his relationship with Ashley. But instead of learning from his mistakes, he'd made a new one, a colossal one.

Des shook his head. "I'm not sure she'll forgive me."

"Maybe. Maybe not. But I'm gonna give you the same advice Riley gave me when I messed up with Mary."

He didn't want to hear it. Maybe this was all for the best. He could go back to being here all alone. Enjoy the peace and quiet. No endless chatter. No calorie-laden baked goods. What was he thinking? He'd been in hell since he'd messed up with Natalie. "What's that?"

Brody raised his eyebrows. "His advice? He told me to tell her I loved her and that I had messed up."

"And that worked?" Skepticism laced his tone. He had a right to it because he couldn't imagine Brody saying anything near as nasty as he had.

"It did and I thank God for Mary and Elliott. I work every day to deserve the family we've created." He shook his head. "I always thought I wanted to be alone, thought it was better not to take that risk of getting hurt. I'm here to tell you that's a load of hogwash. The best thing I did was to stop worrying about what could happen and make today happen. Embrace all the good stuff I have right now and let the future take care of itself."

Natalie opened the door to the Loon Lake General Store and the bell hanging from the casing tinkled. Something about that old-fashioned sound always made her smile, which was no easy task these past three days. Would she ever be able to smile and mean it? Good thing she'd had a lot of practice grinning at strangers who made comments about Sam.

Tavie glanced up from the magazine she had spread out on the wooden counter. "No Sam today?"

"He went to the library with Addie and Teddy Miller. They were having a Christmas party for the younger kids. He and Teddy are going to help pass out gifts. It's part of my effort to teach Sam about the true meaning of Christmas." Natalie pulled off her gloves and unbuttoned the top two buttons of her red parka. "I decided to use the alone time to run some errands and check to be sure Ogle is still planning to play Santa at the carnival tonight."

Tavie touched her helmet of teased and sprayed hair. "He wouldn't miss it."

"Great." Natalie twisted her gloves between her hands. "I've decided to let Sam line up and sit on Santa's lap by himself. I know I have to start letting him do things on his own, but it's hard."

Tavie nodded in agreement. "Do you think encouraging him to do things by himself will help him adapt to using his tablet?"

"That's the plan." She didn't mention how he'd started to use it but had lost interest when she and Des broke up. Broke up? Had they even had a real relationship? She'd been falling in love and he'd been…what? Having good sex? Bitterness coated her stomach.

As if sensing Natalie's distress, Tavie reached across the counter and patted her arm. "Don't you fret. Ogle knows what to do. Sam will be in good hands."

Natalie didn't correct the other woman's misconception. She loved Tavie, but knew better than to divulge certain things. The older woman would be on an all-out campaign to reunite her and Des. "Thanks. He might not believe in Santa too much longer. I want this to go well since I convinced him Santa knows how much he likes LEGOs."

"Yeah. When my grandkids were that age they couldn't get enough of 'em."

"Sam has been begging for the bigger, more complicated kits. Teddy has some and the two sit for hours, building things."

"Does he know which one he wants so I can tell Ogle?"

"He had wanted the airport but…uh…I think he may have changed his mind." Yeah, she'd done her best to explain why Des didn't come around anymore. Of course that hadn't stopped Sam from running to the window every time he heard a car or pickup go down the street.

It broke her heart each time he came away from the window disappointed and every time it happened, she convinced herself she hated Des. Then her phone would buzz and her heart would jump into her throat in that moment before she picked it up to check the caller ID. That phone made a liar out of her every damn time.

Tavie was giving her a peculiar look so she cleared her head of such thoughts and managed a semblance of a smile. "We ran into Liam McBride in his fire uniform in the parking lot at the Pic-N-Save yesterday. Liam had been at his niece Fiona's school giving a talk about fire safety. He gave Sam a badge and plastic fire helmet he had in his truck. Sam's eyes got as big as saucers and he was looking up LEGO fire stations when we got home."

"That Liam is such a sweet kid. His ma would be proud to see what a wonderful family man he is. I swear, every time he and Ellie bring the twins in, they've grown twice as big as the previous time."

Natalie nodded, grateful Tavie's attention was focused elsewhere. "Ellie brought them a few times to the church luncheon when I was volunteering."

"I'm so glad the younger generation in this town is carrying on with some of our traditions. Not to mention adding to the population." Tavie gave her a speculative look. "I hear tell you and the lieutenant have been seen together. Mitch Makowski says you three were together at the tree-lighting."

Anxious to avoid Tavie seeing how her heart was shattered into a million tiny pieces, Natalie glanced at her watch. "Look at the time. I really need to run. I told Addie I'd watch Teddy for her this afternoon and

I need to check that the auction items are all in place. You'll remind Ogle about Sam?"

"Sure thing, honey. Don't you worry. I'll have Ogle ask leading questions about them LEGOs."

"Thanks so much for understanding," Natalie said.

She left the store confident that Sam's visit with Santa tonight was taken care of, as were the horses. She'd talked with Brody again this morning, and while he'd reassured her everything was fine, he'd put her off again when she'd suggested coming to help with Augie's care. She'd tried to insist but didn't want to argue with Brody after he'd been so nice and understanding with her. Not accompanying Brody when he went to collect the horses from Des's place had been cowardly on her part, but she'd been too raw.

Plus, she'd feared seeing Des again might weaken her resolve and she'd throw pride to the wind to beg Des to resume their relationship—on his terms. Pride and self-respect were cold comfort during the long nights, but she'd make whatever sacrifices were necessary to see Sam had a secure and stable life.

"Yeah, pride's a bitch when you're alone," she muttered as she started her car.

But she wasn't alone, she reminded herself. She had Sam and all the friends she'd made in her short time in Loon Lake. She'd get through this and maybe someday she'd even find a guy who didn't run from love.

Chapter Eleven

That evening Natalie pulled into the church parking
lot and found a spot. It was still early and people were
just beginning to arrive, but she'd needed to take one
last look at the silent auction items. She'd wanted to be
sure no one had dropped off anything at the last minute.

Besides, keeping busy was her saving grace. It sure
beat sitting alone and sobbing. No, she would save that
particular pastime for the long winter nights after Sam
went to bed.

She got out of the car and pulled her coat closer
around her to protect against the chill as she crossed
the parking lot. Addie had insisted on bringing Sam
with her and Teddy.

Inside the church she went to the room with her auction items on display. She flipped on the switch for the

overhead lighting and froze. Many of the items had been pushed aside to make room...

She shook her head and blinked, but the items didn't disappear. Right there in the middle of the display lay dozens of glass ornaments. Cautiously, as if they might disappear, she stepped closer. On the table was an assortment of the most exquisite ornaments she'd ever seen, each one a miniature stained or blown glass masterpiece.

She glanced around, but she was alone, so she dashed from the room. People were beginning to gather for the indoor activities, but she could see no six-foot-plus lieutenant. Going to the entrance she opened the door and scanned the parking lot. No sign of his truck, either. Her heart squeezed. Des had made the ornaments she'd wanted but hadn't stayed, hadn't wanted to run into her. What did this mean? If not for his absence, she might have gotten her hopes up, but this seemed like a clear sign that he was done with her, with Sam...forever.

Even so, each time a new person entered the building, her heart would stutter. Once word got out about the ornaments Des had made—and she had no doubt he'd made them—people flocked to place auction bids. They hung around to ask about the hippotherapy program and the town's business leaders promised to help get the center back on its feet. Some even encouraged her to consider taking over the administrative side of the business. She promised to consider it.

"Hey, is it true?" Addie came up to her.

Natalie pointed to the table with the ornaments. "See for yourself."

Addie scooted over to get a look. When she turned

back, her eyes were wide and her mouth open. "He did this for you? I take back every bad thing I thought about him."

Dare she allow herself to believe this gesture was for her? "He may have done it for Sam's benefit. He knows how much the horses mean to him."

Addie shook her head. "That's an awful lot of work for a guy who doesn't care. He must've been working day and night to make all these. They're gorgeous."

Natalie brought her fist to her mouth and pressed it there to stifle a sob. Was it true? Or did she want it to be true? "I don't know what to believe."

"Maybe you should talk to him. Find out what it means."

"You're right. He must've dropped these off and left because I've looked all over and haven't seen him."

"Maybe you should look again. I can watch over things in here." Addie gave her a quick hug. "Sam's in line for Santa. Sorry, but we were a little bit late getting here so he's the last one in line, but I kept an eye on him and it was his turn. That's why I came to find you. In case you wanted to go check on him."

"That's fine. Ogle knows what to do." Natalie returned the hug.

Addie's brow furrowed. "What's Ogle got to do with it?"

"He's Santa."

"No, he's not," Addie said. "He helped me unload and carry in the stuff we made for the bake sale."

"What?" Natalie's heart sank, but surely Ogle would have told whoever took his place about Sam.

She hurried to where the children had lined up for

Santa and searched for Sam. He was seated on Santa's lap. She started to rush forward but stopped when she saw that Santa was speaking to Sam, who was grinning and nodding his head. So maybe Ogle did make arrangements.

Santa lifted his head, seemed to zero in on her and caught her gaze. The glued-on bushy eyebrows, moustache and beard obscured his identity, but that gaze made her stomach flutter with recognition. But the memory giving her déjà vu was beyond her reach.

Santa leaned down and spoke into Sam's ear. What was going on? Grinning from ear to ear, Sam nodded, scrambled off Santa's lap and ran toward her.

"Did you tell Santa what you wanted?" She was still confused as to what was going on. And there was something about that Santa…

Sam tugged on her sleeve, pulling her toward one of the empty Sunday schoolrooms.

"Sam? What in the world…?" She glanced down at her son but he giggled and pushed her into the room.

As soon as she stepped into the classroom, Sam scampered off. "Sam, wait! What is—"

She turned and bumped into Santa, who put his hands on her shoulders to steady her and gently push her back into the room. He shut the door and flipped on the overhead lights.

Her gaze met his and recognition flooded into her. "Des?"

He nodded and yanked off the hat and pulled down the white beard. Those dark eyes glittered as he looked at her.

"I…I…" She shook her head but couldn't form a co-

herent thought. This was all too much for her to process. "I don't understand. What's going on? Why are
you dressed as Santa?"

"I convinced Ogle to let me take over for him tonight."

"Why?" She couldn't imagine why Des would dress
up as Santa.

"Because I wanted to prove to you how much I've
changed since we last spoke."

"You dressed up as Santa for me?"

"Everything I did was for you, Natalie. I made the
ornaments for you."

"But I told you I didn't expect you to make any. I
understand and respect why you didn't want to make
them." She shook her head. "I never should have tried
to force you to begin with. I was wrong."

"But don't you see? I'm grateful you did because
you've replaced my bad memories of Christmas with
good ones."

"You mean that?" She tentatively reached out her
hand to touch him, assure herself he was real—and
wearing a Santa suit, of all things. He captured her
hand in his and curled his fingers around it, his thumb
stroking her palm. She leaned toward him, drawn in,
despite her caution.

"I still can't believe you made ornaments," she said
and her voice sounded breathless even to her own ears.
She was beginning to understand the enormity of what
was happening.

"Those don't even begin to express how sorry I am."

"They don't?"

"I acted like…" He squeezed her hand. Swallowing

audibly, he started again, "I acted like an ass. Can you ever forgive me for the way I behaved and those things I said? I swear I didn't mean any of it. I was running scared. My—" He swallowed again. "My feelings for you and Sam scared me. Huh, they still do, but that's okay because being without the two of you scares me even more. You and Sam are my whole life, Natalie. I've been so miserable without you. I can't eat. I can't sleep. I want to spend the rest of my life with you." He rubbed the back of his neck. "Heck, I'm not even sure if that's long enough. I want forever and ever. Tell me I'm not too late."

"Oh, Des, I've been miserable, too," she cried and threw herself against him.

He made an impatient noise and reached under the Santa suit and pulled out the pillow he'd had to use as padding. Then he put his arms around her, hugging her close.

"Shh, don't cry. Please. I don't want to make you cry," he whispered. "I love you. Please believe me when I say it. I love you and Sam more than I ever thought possible. What I felt for Ashley is nothing compared to what I feel for you."

"I love you, too." She choked on a sob and clung to him.

He brought his hands up to cup her face and kissed her. He kissed her as if his life depended on what their lips were doing, pouring everything he ever was and ever would be into the kiss.

After long minutes he lifted his mouth and sucked in air. Resting his forehead against hers, he drew in a deep breath and shuddered. "I told Sam I had something for you but I needed his permission to give it to you because he's a part of this, of us."

"What did you need Sam's permission for?" She was afraid to hope but couldn't prevent it from seeping into her.

He pulled a small black box out of the pocket of his pants.

"Santa pants have pockets?" That's what she was getting from all this? By concentrating on the mundane, she hoped to manage her expectations in case that box didn't contain what she prayed it did.

"Fortunately, these do." He opened the box. Nestled inside was a sparkling solitaire diamond. He cleared his throat. "I told Sam I wanted to be his dad and to marry you, but I would need his permission for both."

"You did?"

Des nodded. "I did. And he gave me an enthusiastic thumbs-up. I told him I hoped his mom would be as agreeable."

He dropped to one knee. "Natalie Pierce, will you marry me? I think I fell in love with you the day you came barging into my barn and my life with your baked goods and your big blue eyes. I was lost the moment you smiled and I saw that crooked tooth."

She put her hand over her mouth. "My snaggle tooth."

He reached out and took her hand away from her mouth, bringing it to his own. He kissed her palm, then pressed her hand against his chest. "If not for that tooth, I would have turned away, convinced you were too good for the likes of me. But that tooth told me you were real and drove me crazy thinking that maybe I had a shot at the most beautiful and loving woman I'd ever met."

"That silly tooth did all that?"

"That and the way you clutched your son's hand. I didn't know the particulars at the time, but that act started thawing something that had been frozen in me for a long, long time."

"And here I thought it was my cookies that hooked you."

"Those, too." He grinned and pulled her closer. "Especially those little green ones with the chocolate on them."

"And the sprinkles," she whispered and snuggled against his shoulder. Amazing how she could go from despair to happiness in such a short span.

"Sam put the sprinkles on so I definitely can't forget those."

She pulled away to look at him. "Sam has challenges ahead of him."

His gaze seemed to be asking for her trust. "And we'll give him a solid, loving home life so that he will be able to meet all of those challenges head-on. We'll equip him and his future brothers and sisters with the skills necessary to conquer the world."

"Brothers and sisters?" She hadn't even thought that far ahead. Not tonight, anyway.

"No?"

She smiled and sniffed. "Yes, definitely yes. Gotta fill up that house."

"With kids and animals."

"Oh, no!" Her jaw dropped. "Animals… The horses. I… They—"

"Are safe at my place. I wouldn't let Brody take them. I couldn't let go of that link to you and Sam." Moisture gathered in his eyes as if the thought brought him pain. He blushed. "I may have done some begging. The swine laughed and said it was good to get in some practice before I came to see you."

"No wonder Brody wouldn't let us come and see Augie." She laughed. "I need to apologize to him for all the things I thought each time he made an excuse and put us off. So, was it Brody who suggested you play Santa?"

He shook his head and hugged her closer. "Nope. I came up with that one myself. I knew Ogle always played Santa, so I contacted him this afternoon."

Her eyes widened because she knew you couldn't involve Ogle in anything without involving his wife. "You involved Tavie?"

"I was desperate," he admitted with a sheepish expression. "I'm nothing without you and Sam."

"But you're everything to Sam and me," she vowed and stood on tiptoe to kiss him.

After they came up for air, he rested his forehead against hers. "I'm going to be there for you and Sam for the rest of my life. You have my word on that."

Her heart expanded until it hurt to breathe. "Sounds exactly like my kind of happily-ever-after."

"Mine, too." He took her hand and intertwined his fingers with hers. "Should we go and find Sam and let him know that you've agreed to bless my heart forever?"

* * * * *

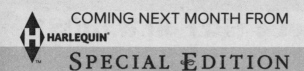

Get 4 FREE REWARDS!

We'll send you 2 FREE Books plus 2 FREE Mystery Gifts.

Harlequin® Special Edition books feature heroines finding the balance between their work life and personal life on the way to finding true love.

FREE Value Over **$20**

YES! Please send me 2 FREE Harlequin® Special Edition novels and my 2 FREE gifts (gifts are worth about $10 retail). After receiving them, if I don't wish to receive any more books, I can return the shipping statement marked "cancel." If I don't cancel, I will receive 6 brand-new novels every month and be billed just $4.99 per book in the U.S. or $5.74 per book in Canada. That's a savings of at least 12% off the cover price! It's quite a bargain! Shipping and handling is just 50¢ per book in the U.S. and $1.25 per book in Canada.* I understand that accepting the 2 free books and gifts places me under no obligation to buy anything. I can always return a shipment and cancel at any time. The free books and gifts are mine to keep no matter what I decide.

235/335 HDN GNMP

Name (please print)

Address   Apt. #

City   State/Province   Zip/Postal Code

Mail to the **Reader Service:**
IN U.S.A.: P.O. Box 1341, Buffalo, NY 14240-8531
IN CANADA: P.O. Box 603, Fort Erie, Ontario L2A 5X3

Want to try 2 free books from another series? Call 1-800-873-8635 or visit www.ReaderService.com.

"Amanda, I didn't mean to upset you. I don't ever want to
do anything that scares you."

She sucked in a deep, ragged breath, looking so
terribly lost and sad. Her eyelids fluttered open. She
stared straight ahead, talking to his chest.

"You don't understand, Blake. There are days when...
when everything scares me." Her voice was barely above
a whisper. His heart jumped. He thought of that first day,
when she ended up unconscious in his arms.

Everything scares me.

She'd kicked her shoes off earlier, and in her bare
feet the top of her head barely reached his shoulders. He
put his fingers under her chin and gently tipped her head
back.

He wanted to kiss this woman.

Wait. What?

No. That would be wild. He couldn't kiss her. Shouldn't. But how could he not?

Her hair tumbled off her shoulders and down her back in golden curls. Before he knew it, his free hand was slowly twisting into those curls. She didn't pull away. Didn't look away. He lowered his head until his face was just above hers. He felt her breath on his skin. She smelled like citrus and spice and blueberries and red wine. Her lips parted and she stared at him with her enormous eyes.

"I swear I don't want to scare you, Amanda. But… may I kiss you?" His voice was a raw whisper. "Please let me kiss you."

His words came out as a plea. He'd never begged for anything before in his life. But here he was, begging this sweet woman for a kiss. Ready to drop to his knees if that was what it took. He heard his father's voice in his head, mocking his weakness. That was when he started to straighten, started to come to his senses. Then he heard her whispered answer.

"Yes."

Was there any sweeter word in the world? Adrenaline surged through his body, and his hand tightened in her hair. His eyes opened to meet those two oceans of blue. Dangerous blue. Deep enough to drown in.

She was frightened, but she was trusting him. And that realization scared him to death.

Don't miss It Started at Christmas… *by Jo McNally, available December 2019 wherever Harlequin® Special Edition books and ebooks are sold.*

Harlequin.com

Looking for more satisfying love stories
with community and family at their core?

Check out **Harlequin®** Special Edition
and **Love Inspired®** books!

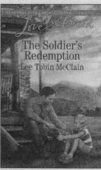

New books available every month!

CONNECT WITH US AT:

Facebook.com/groups/HarlequinConnection

Facebook.com/HarlequinBooks

Twitter.com/HarlequinBooks

Instagram.com/HarlequinBooks

Pinterest.com/HarlequinBooks

ReaderService.com

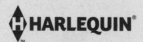

**ROMANCE WHEN
YOU NEED IT**

HFGENRE2018